I0535213

Four Georges by William Makepeace Thackeray

The great author of Vanity Fair and The Luck Of Barry Lyndon was born in India in 1811.

At age 5 his father died and his mother sent him back to England. His education was of the best but he himself seemed unable to apply his talents to a rigorous work ethic.

However, once he harnessed his talents the works flowed in novels, articles, short stories, sketches and lectures.

Sadly, his personal life was rather more difficult. After a few years of marriage his wife began to suffer from depression and over the years became detached from reality. Thackeray himself suffered from ill health later in his life and the one pursuit that kept him moving forward was that of writing. In his life time, he was placed second only to Dickens. High praise indeed.

Index of Contents

THE GEORGES

THE POEMS

As the statues of these beloved Monarchs are to be put up in the Parliament palace—we have been favoured by a young lady (connected with the Court) with copies of the inscriptions which are to be engraven under the images of those Stars of Brunswick.

GEORGE I—STAR OF BRUNSWICK

He preferred Hanover to England,
He preferred two hideous Mistresses
To a beautiful and innocent Wife.
He hated Arts and despised Literature;
But He liked train-oil in his salads,
And gave an enlightened patronage to bad oysters.
And he had Walpole as a Minister:
Consistent in his Preference for every kind of Corruption.

GEORGE II

In most things I did as my father had done,
I was false to my wife and I hated my son:

My spending was small and my avarice much,
My kingdom was English, my heart was High Dutch:

At Dettingen fight I was known not to blench
I butchered the Scotch, and I bearded the French:

I neither had morals, nor manners, nor wit;
I wasn't much missed when I died in a fit.

Here set up my statue, and make it complete—With
Pitt on his knees at my dirty old feet.

GEORGE III

Give me a royal niche—it is my due,
The virtuousest king the realm e'er knew.

I, through a decent reputable life,
Was constant to plain food and a plain wife.

Ireland I risked, and lost America;
But dined on legs of mutton every day.

My brain, perhaps, might be a feeble part;
But yet I think I had an English heart.

When all the kings were prostrate, I alone
Stood face to face against Napoleon;

Nor ever could the ruthless Frenchman forge

A fetter for Old England and Old George:

I let loose flaming Nelson on his fleets;
I met his troops with Wellesley's bayonets.

Triumphant waved my flag on land and sea:
Where was the king in Europe like to me?

Monarchs exiled found shelter on my shores;
My bounty rescued kings and emperors.

But what boots victory by land or sea?
What boots that kings found refuge at my knee?

I was a conqueror, but yet not proud;
And careless, even though Napoleon bow'd.

The rescued kings came kiss my garments' hem:
The rescued kings I never heeded them.

My guns roar'd triumph, but I never heard:
All England thrilled with joy, I never stirred.

What care had I of pomp, or fame, or power,—
A crazy old blind man in Windsor Tower?

GEORGIUS ULTIMUS

He left an example for age and for youth
To avoid.
He never acted well by Man or Woman,
And was as false to his Mistress as to his Wife.
He deserted his Friends and his Principles.
He was so ignorant that he could scarcely Spell;
But he had some Skill in Cutting out Coats,
And an undeniable Taste for Cookery.
He built the Palaces of Brighton and of Buckingham,
And for these Qualities and Proofs of Genius,
An admiring Aristocracy
Christened him the "First Gentleman in Europe".
Friends, respect the King whose Statue is here,
And the generous Aristocracy who admired him.

SKETCHES OF MANNERS, MORALS, COURT AND TOWN LIFE

A very few years since, I knew familiarly a lady, who had been asked in marriage by Horace Walpole, who had been patted on the head by George I. This lady had knocked at Johnson's door; had been intimate with Fox, the beautiful Georgina of Devonshire, and that brilliant Whig society of the reign of George III; had known the Duchess of Queensberry, the patroness of Gay and Prior, the admired young beauty of the Court of Queen Anne. I often thought as I took my kind old friend's hand, how with it I held on to the old society of wits and men of the world. I could travel back for sevenscore years of time—have glimpses of Brummell, Selwyn, Chesterfield and the men of pleasure; of Walpole and Conway; of Johnson, Reynolds, Goldsmith; of North, Chatham, Newcastle; of the fair maids of honour of George II's Court; of the German retainers of George I's; where Addison was secretary of state; where Dick Steele held a place; whither the great Marlborough came with his fiery spouse; when Pope, and Swift, and Bolingbroke yet lived and wrote. Of a society so vast, busy, brilliant, it is impossible in four brief chapters to give a complete notion; but we may peep here and there into that bygone world of the Georges, see what they and their Courts were like; glance at the people round about them; look at past manners, fashions, pleasures, and contrast them with our own. I have to say thus much by way of preface, because the subject of these lectures has been misunderstood, and I have been taken to task for not having given grave historical treatises, which it never was my intention to attempt. Not about battles, about politics, about statesmen and measures of state, did I ever think to lecture you: but to sketch the manners and life of the old world; to amuse for a few hours with talk about the old society; and, with the result of many a day's and night's pleasant reading, to try and wile away a few winter evenings for my hearers.

Among the German princes who sat under Luther at Wittenberg, was Duke Ernest of Celle, whose younger son, William of Lüneburg, was the progenitor of the illustrious Hanoverian house at present reigning in Great Britain. Duke William held his Court at Celle, a little town of ten thousand people that lies on the railway line between Hamburg and Hanover, in the midst of great plains of sand, upon the river Aller. When Duke William had it, it was a very humble wood-built place, with a great brick church, which he sedulously frequented, and in which he and others of his house lie buried. He was a very religious lord, and called William the Pious by his small circle of subjects, over whom he ruled till fate deprived him both of sight and reason. Sometimes, in his latter days, the good duke had glimpses of mental light, when he would bid his musicians play the psalm-tunes which he loved. One thinks of a descendant of his, two hundred years afterwards, blind, old, and lost of wits, singing Handel in Windsor Tower.

William the Pious had fifteen children, eight daughters and seven sons, who, as the property left among them was small, drew lots to determine which one of them should marry, and continue the stout race of the Guelphs. The lot fell on Duke George, the sixth brother. The others remained single, or contracted left-handed marriages after the princely fashion of those days. It is a queer picture—that of the old prince dying in his little wood-built capital, and his seven sons tossing up which should inherit and transmit the crown of Brentford. Duke George, the lucky prizeman, made the tour of Europe, during which he visited the Court of Queen Elizabeth; and in the year 1617, came back and settled at Zell, with a wife out of Darmstadt. His remaining brothers all kept their house at Zell, for economy's sake. And presently, in due course, they all died—all the honest dukes; Ernest, and Christian, and Augustus, and Magnus, and George, and John—and they are buried in the brick church of Brentford yonder, by the sandy banks of the Aller.

Dr. Vehse gives a pleasant glimpse of the way of life of our dukes in Zell. "When the trumpeter on the tower has blown," Duke Christian orders—viz. at nine o'clock in the morning, and four in the evening, every one must be present at meals, and those who are not must go without. None of the servants, unless it be a knave who has been ordered to ride out, shall eat or drink in the kitchen or cellar; or, without special leave, fodder his horses at the prince's cost. When the meal is served in the Court-room, a page shall go round and bid every one be quiet and orderly, forbidding all cursing, swearing, and rudeness; all throwing about of bread, bones, or roast, or pocketing of the same. Every morning, at seven, the squires shall have their morning soup, along with which, and dinner, they shall be served with their under-drink—every morning, except Friday morning, when there was sermon, and no drink. Every evening they shall have their beer, and at night their sleep-drink. The butler is especially warned not to allow noble or simple to go into the cellar: wine shall only be served at the prince's or councillor's table; and every Monday, the honest old Duke Christian ordains the accounts shall be ready, and the expenses in the kitchen, the wine and beer cellar, the bakehouse and stable, made out.

Duke George, the marrying duke, did not stop at home to partake of the beer and wine, and the sermons. He went about fighting wherever there was profit to be had. He served as general in the army of the circle of Lower Saxony, the Protestant army; then he went over to the emperor, and fought in his armies in Germany and Italy; and when Gustavus Adolphus appeared in Germany, George took service as a Swedish general, and seized the Abbey of Hildesheim, as his share of the plunder. Here, in the year 1641, Duke George died, leaving four sons behind him, from the youngest of whom descend our royal Georges.

Under these children of Duke George, the old God-fearing, simple ways of Zell appear to have gone out of mode. The second brother was constantly visiting Venice, and leading a jolly, wicked life there. It was the most jovial of all places at the end of the seventeenth century; and military men, after a campaign, rushed thither, as the warriors of the Allies rushed to Paris in 1814, to gamble, and rejoice, and partake of all sorts of godless delights. This prince, then, loving Venice and its pleasures, brought Italian singers and dancers back with him to quiet old Zell; and, worse still, demeaned himself by marrying a French lady of birth quite inferior to his own—Eleanor d'Olbreuse, from whom our queen is descended. Eleanor had a pretty daughter, who inherited a great fortune, which inflamed her cousin, George Louis of Hanover, with a desire to marry her; and so, with her beauty and her riches, she came to a sad end.

It is too long to tell how the four sons of Duke George divided his territories amongst them, and how, finally, they came into possession of the son of the youngest of the four. In this generation the Protestant faith was very nearly extinguished in the family: and then where should we in England have gone for a king? The third brother also took delight in Italy, where the priests converted him and his Protestant chaplain too. Mass was said in Hanover once more; and Italian soprani piped their Latin rhymes in place of the hymns which William the Pious and Dr. Luther sang. Louis XIV gave this and other converts a splendid pension. Crowds of Frenchmen and brilliant French fashions came into his Court. It is incalculable how much that royal bigwig cost Germany. Every prince imitated the French king, and had his Versailles, his Wilhelmshöhe or Ludwigslust; his court and its splendours; his gardens laid out with statues; his fountains, and waterworks, and Tritons; his actors, and dancers, and singers, and fiddlers; his harem, with its inhabitants; his diamonds and duchies for these latter; his enormous festivities, his gaming-tables, tournaments, masquerades, and banquets lasting a week long, for which the people paid with their money, when the poor wretches had it; with their bodies and very blood when they had none; being sold in thousands by their lords and masters, who gaily dealt in soldiers, staked a regiment upon the red at the gambling-table; swapped a battalion against a dancing-girl's diamond necklace; and, as it were, pocketed their people.

As one views Europe, through contemporary books of travel in the early part of the last century, the landscape is awful—wretched wastes, beggarly and plundered; half-burned cottages and trembling peasants gathering piteous harvests; gangs of such tramping along with bayonets behind them, and corporals with canes and cats-of-nine-tails to flog them to barracks. By these passes my lord's gilt carriage floundering through the ruts, as he swears at the postilions, and toils on to the Residenz. Hard by, but away from the noise and brawling of the citizens and buyers, is Wilhelmslust or Ludwigsruhe, or Monbijou, or Versailles—it scarcely matters which—near to the city, shut out by woods from the beggared country, the enormous, hideous, gilded, monstrous marble palace, where the prince is, and the Court, and the trim gardens, and huge fountains, and the forest where the ragged peasants are beating the game in (it is death to them to touch a feather); and the jolly hunt sweeps by with its uniform of crimson and gold; and the prince gallops ahead puffing his royal horn; and his lords and mistresses ride after him; and the stag is pulled down; and the grand huntsman gives the knife in the midst of a chorus of bugles; and 'tis time the Court go home to dinner; and our noble traveller, it may be the Baron of Pöllnitz, or the Count de Königsmarck, or the excellent Chevalier de Seingalt, sees the procession gleaming through the trim avenues of the wood, and hastens to the inn, and sends his noble name to the marshal of the Court. Then our nobleman arrays himself in green and gold, or pink and silver, in the richest Paris mode, and is introduced by the chamberlain, and makes his bow to the jolly prince, and the gracious princess; and is presented to the chief lords and ladies, and then comes supper and a bank at faro, where he loses or wins a thousand pieces by daylight. If it is a German Court, you may add not a little drunkenness to this picture of high life; but German, or French, or Spanish, if you can see out of your palace-windows beyond the trim-cut forest vistas, misery is lying outside; hunger is stalking about the bare villages, listlessly following precarious husbandry; ploughing stony fields with starved cattle; or fearfully taking in scanty harvests. Augustus is fat and jolly on his throne; he can knock down an ox, and eat one almost; his mistress Aurora von Königsmarck is the loveliest, the wittiest creature; his diamonds are the biggest and most brilliant in the world, and his feasts as splendid as those of Versailles. As for Louis the Great, he is more than mortal. Lift up your glances respectfully, and mark him eyeing Madame de Fontanges or Madame de Montespan from under his sublime periwig, as he passes through the great gallery where Villars and Vendôme, and Berwick, and Bossuet, and Massillon are waiting. Can Court be more splendid; nobles and knights more gallant and superb; ladies more lovely? A grander monarch, or a more miserable starved wretch than the peasant his subject, you cannot look on. Let us bear both these types in mind, if we wish to estimate the old society properly. Remember the glory and the chivalry? Yes! Remember the grace and beauty, the splendour and lofty politeness; the gallant courtesy of Fontenoy, where the French line bids the gentlemen of the English guard to fire first; the noble constancy of the old king and Villars his general, who fits out the last army with the last crown-piece from the treasury, and goes to meet the enemy and die or conquer for France at Denain. But round all that royal splendour lies a nation enslaved and ruined: there are people robbed of their rights—communities laid waste—faith, justice, commerce trampled upon, and wellnigh destroyed—nay, in the very centre of royalty itself, what horrible stains and meanness, crime and shame! It is but to a silly harlot that some of the noblest gentlemen, and some of the proudest women in the world, are bowing down; it is the price of a miserable province that the king ties in diamonds round his mistress's white neck. In the first half of the last century, I say, this is going on all Europe over. Saxony is a waste as well as Picardy or Artois; and Versailles is only larger and not worse than Herrenhausen.

It was the first Elector of Hanover who made the fortunate match which bestowed the race of Hanoverian Sovereigns upon us Britons. Nine years after Charles Stuart lost his head, his niece Sophia, one of many children of another luckless dethroned sovereign, the Elector Palatine, married Ernest

Augustus of Brunswick, and brought the reversion to the crown of the three kingdoms in her scanty trousseau. One of the handsomest, the most cheerful, sensible, shrewd, accomplished of women was Sophia,(186) daughter of poor Frederick, the winter king of Bohemia. The other daughters of lovely, unhappy Elizabeth Stuart went off into the Catholic Church; this one, luckily for her family, remained, I cannot say faithful to the Reformed Religion, but at least she adopted no other. An agent of the French king's, Gourville, a convert himself, strove to bring her and her husband to a sense of the truth; and tells us that he one day asked madame the Duchess of Hanover, of what religion her daughter was, then a pretty girl of thirteen years old. The duchess replied that the princess was of no religion as yet. They were waiting to know of what religion her husband would be, Protestant or Catholic, before instructing her! And the Duke of Hanover having heard all Gourville's proposal, said that a change would be advantageous to his house, but that he himself was too old to change.

This shrewd woman had such keen eyes that she knew how to shut them upon occasion, and was blind to many faults which it appeared that her husband the Bishop of Osnaburg and Duke of Hanover committed. He loved to take his pleasure like other sovereigns—was a merry prince, fond of dinner and the bottle; liked to go to Italy, as his brothers had done before him; and we read how he jovially sold 6,700 of his Hanoverians to the seigniory of Venice. They went bravely off to the Morea, under command of Ernest's son, Prince Max, and only 1,400 of them ever came home again. The German princes sold a good deal of this kind of stock. You may remember how George III's Government purchased Hessians, and the use we made of them during the War of Independence.

The ducats Duke Ernest got for his soldiers he spent in a series of the most brilliant entertainments. Nevertheless, the jovial prince was economical, and kept a steady eye upon his own interests. He achieved the electoral dignity for himself: he married his eldest son George to his beautiful cousin of Zell; and sending his sons out in command of armies to fight—now on this side, now on that—he lived on, taking his pleasure, and scheming his schemes, a merry, wise prince enough, not, I fear, a moral prince, of which kind we shall have but very few specimens in the course of these lectures.

Ernest Augustus had seven children in all, some of whom were scapegraces, and rebelled against the parental system of primogeniture and non-division of property which the Elector ordained. "Gustchen," the Electress writes about her second son:—"Poor Gus is thrust out, and his father will give him no more keep. I laugh in the day, and cry all night about it; for I am a fool with my children." Three of the six died fighting against Turks, Tartars, Frenchmen. One of them conspired, revolted, fled to Rome, leaving an agent behind him, whose head was taken off. The daughter, of whose early education we have made mention, was married to the Elector of Brandenburg, and so her religion settled finally on the Protestant side.

A niece of the Electress Sophia—who had been made to change her religion, and marry the Duke of Orleans, brother of the French king; a woman whose honest heart was always with her friends and dear old Deutschland, though her fat little body was confined at Paris or Marly, or Versailles—has left us, in her enormous correspondence (part of which has been printed in German and French), recollections of the Electress, and of George her son. Elizabeth Charlotte was at Osnaburg when George was born (1660). She narrowly escaped a whipping for being in the way on that auspicious day. She seems not to have liked little George, nor George grown up; and represents him as odiously hard, cold, and silent. Silent he may have been: not a jolly prince like his father before him, but a prudent, quiet, selfish potentate, going his own way, managing his own affairs, and understanding his own interests remarkably well.

In his father's lifetime, and at the head of the Hanover forces of 8,000 or 10,000 men, George served the Emperor, on the Danube against Turks, at the siege of Vienna, in Italy, and on the Rhine. When he succeeded to the Electorate, he handled its affairs with great prudence and dexterity. He was very much liked by his people of Hanover. He did not show his feelings much, but he cried heartily on leaving them; as they used for joy when he came back. He showed an uncommon prudence and coolness of behaviour when he came into his kingdom; exhibiting no elation; reasonably doubtful whether he should not be turned out some day; looking upon himself only as a lodger, and making the most of his brief tenure of St. James's and Hampton Court; plundering, it is true, somewhat, and dividing amongst his German followers; but what could be expected of a sovereign who at home could sell his subjects at so many ducats per head, and made no scruple in so disposing of them? I fancy a considerable shrewdness, prudence, and even moderation in his ways. The German Protestant was a cheaper, and better, and kinder king than the Catholic Stuart in whose chair he sat, and so far loyal to England, that he let England govern herself.

Having these lectures in view I made it my business to visit that ugly cradle in which our Georges were nursed. The old town of Hanover must look still pretty much as in the time when George Louis left it. The gardens and pavilions of Herrenhausen are scarce changed since the day when the stout old Electress Sophia fell down in her last walk there, preceding but by a few weeks to the tomb James II's daughter, whose death made way for the Brunswick Stuarts in England.

The two first royal Georges, and their father, Ernest Augustus, had quite royal notions regarding marriage; and Louis XIV and Charles II scarce distinguished themselves more at Versailles or St. James's, than these German sultans in their little city on the banks of the Leine. You may see at Herrenhausen the very rustic theatre in which the Platens danced and performed masques, and sang before the Elector and his sons. There are the very fauns and dryads of stone still glimmering through the branches, still grinning and piping their ditties of no tone, as in the days when painted nymphs hung garlands round them; appeared under their leafy arcades with gilt crooks, guiding rams with gilt horns; descended from "machines" in the guise of Diana or Minerva; and delivered immense allegorical compliments to the princes returned home from the campaign.

That was a curious state of morals and politics in Europe; a queer consequence of the triumph of the monarchical principle. Feudalism was beaten down. The nobility, in its quarrels with the crown, had pretty well succumbed, and the monarch was all in all. He became almost divine: the proudest and most ancient gentry of the land did menial service for him. Who should carry Louis XIV's candle when he went to bed? What prince of the blood should hold the king's shirt when his Most Christian Majesty changed that garment?—the French memoirs of the seventeenth century are full of such details and squabbles. The tradition is not yet extinct in Europe. Any of you who were present, as myriads were, at that splendid pageant, the opening of our Crystal Palace in London, must have seen two noble lords, great officers of the household, with ancient pedigrees, with embroidered coats, and stars on their breasts and wands in their hands, walking backwards for near the space of a mile, while the royal procession made its progress. Shall we wonder—shall we be angry—shall we laugh at these old-world ceremonies? View them as you will, according to your mood; and with scorn or with respect, or with anger and sorrow, as your temper leads you. Up goes Gesler's hat upon the pole. Salute that symbol of sovereignty with heartfelt awe; or with a sulky shrug of acquiescence, or with a grinning obeisance; or with a stout rebellious No—clap your own beaver down on your pate, and refuse to doff it, to that spangled velvet and flaunting feather. I make no comment upon the spectators' behaviour; all I say is, that Gesler's cap is still up in the market-place of Europe, and not a few folks are still kneeling to it.

Put clumsy, High Dutch statues in place of the marbles of Versailles: fancy Herrenhausen waterworks in place of those of Marly: spread the tables with Schweinskopf, Specksuppe, Leberkuchen, and the like delicacies, in place of the French cuisine; and fancy Frau von Kielmansegge dancing with Count Kammerjunker Quirini, or singing French songs with the most awful German accent: imagine a coarse Versailles, and we have a Hanover before us. "I am now got into the region of beauty," writes Mary Wortley, from Hanover in 1716; "all the women have literally rosy cheeks, snowy foreheads and necks, jet eyebrows, to which may generally be added coal-black hair. These perfections never leave them to the day of their death, and have a very fine effect by candlelight; but I could wish they were handsome with a little variety. They resemble one another as Mrs. Salmon's Court of Great Britain, and are in as much danger of melting away by too nearly approaching the fire." The sly Mary Wortley saw this painted seraglio of the first George at Hanover, the year after his accession to the British throne. There were great doings and feasts there. Here Lady Mary saw George II too. "I can tell you, without flattery or partiality," she says, "that our young prince has all the accomplishments that it is possible to have at his age, with an air of sprightliness and understanding, and a something so very engaging in his behaviour that needs not the advantage of his rank to appear charming." I find elsewhere similar panegyrics upon Frederick Prince of Wales, George II's son; and upon George III, of course, and upon George IV in an eminent degree. It was the rule to be dazzled by princes, and people's eyes winked quite honestly at that royal radiance.

The Electoral Court of Hanover was numerous—pretty well paid, as times went; above all, paid with a regularity which few other European Courts could boast of. Perhaps you will be amused to know how the Electoral Court was composed. There were the princes of the house in the first class; in the second, the single field-marshal of the army (the contingent was 18,000, Pöllnitz says, and the Elector had other 14,000 troops in his pay). Then follow, in due order, the authorities civil and military, the working privy councillors, the generals of cavalry and infantry, in the third class; the high chamberlain, high marshals of the Court, high masters of the horse, the major-generals of cavalry and infantry, in the fourth class; down to the majors, the Hofjunkers or pages, the secretaries or assessors, of the tenth class, of whom all were noble.

We find the master of the horse had 1,090 thalers of pay; the high chamberlain, 2,000—a thaler being about three shillings of our money. There were two chamberlains, and one for the princess; five gentlemen of the chamber, and five gentlemen ushers; eleven pages and personages to educate these young noblemen—such as a governor, a preceptor, a Fechtmeister, or fencing-master, and a dancing ditto, this latter with a handsome salary of 400 thalers. There were three body and Court physicians, with 800 and 500 thalers; a Court barber, 600 thalers; a Court organist; two Musikanten; four French fiddlers; twelve trumpeters, and a bugler; so that there was plenty of music, profane and pious, in Hanover. There were ten chamber waiters, and twenty-four lackeys in livery; a maitre-d'hôtel, and attendants of the kitchen; a French cook; a body cook; ten cooks; six cooks' assistants; two Braten masters, or masters of the roast—(one fancies enormous spits turning slowly, and the honest masters of the roast beladling the dripping); a pastry baker; a pie baker; and finally, three scullions, at the modest remuneration of eleven thalers. In the sugar-chamber there were four pastry-cooks (for the ladies, no doubt); seven officers in the wine and beer cellars; four bread bakers; and five men in the plate-room. There were 600 horses in the Serene stables—no less than twenty teams of princely carriage horses, eight to a team; sixteen coachmen; fourteen postilions; nineteen ostlers; thirteen helps, besides smiths, carriage-masters, horse-doctors, and other attendants of the stable. The female attendants were not so numerous: I grieve to find but a dozen or fourteen of them about the Electoral premises, and only two washerwomen for all the Court. These functionaries had not so much to do as in the present age. I own to finding a pleasure in these small-beer chronicles. I like to people the old world, with its everyday figures and inhabitants—not so much with heroes fighting immense battles and inspiring repulsed battalions to engage; or statesmen locked up in darkling cabinets and meditating ponderous laws or dire conspiracies—as with people occupied with their every-day work or pleasure: my lord and lady hunting in the forest, or dancing in the Court, or bowing to their serene highnesses as they pass in to dinner; John Cook and his procession bringing the meal from the kitchen; the jolly butlers bearing in the flagons from the cellar; the stout coachman driving the ponderous gilt wagon, with eight cream-coloured horses in housings of scarlet velvet and morocco leather; a postilion on the leaders, and a pair or a half-dozen of running footmen scudding along by the side of the vehicle, with conical caps, long silver-headed maces, which they poised as they ran, and splendid jackets laced all over with silver and gold. I fancy the citizens' wives and their daughters looking out from the balconies; and the burghers over their beer and mumm, rising up, cap in hand, as the cavalcade passes through the town with torchbearers, trumpeters blowing their lusty cheeks out, and squadrons of jack-booted life-guardsmen, girt with shining cuirasses, and bestriding thundering chargers, escorting his highness's coach from Hanover to Herrenhausen: or halting, mayhap, at Madame Platen's country house of Monplaisir, which lies half-way between the summer palace and the Residenz.

In the good old times of which I am treating, whilst common men were driven off by herds, and sold to fight the emperor's enemies on the Danube, or to bayonet King Louis's troops of common men on the Rhine, noblemen passed from Court to Court, seeking service with one prince or the other, and naturally taking command of the ignoble vulgar of soldiery which battled and died almost without hope of promotion. Noble adventurers travelled from Court to Court in search of employment; not merely noble males, but noble females too; and if these latter were beauties, and obtained the favourable notice of princes, they stopped in the Courts, became the favourites of their serene or royal highnesses; and received great sums of money and splendid diamonds; and were promoted to be duchesses, marchionesses, and the like; and did not fall much in public esteem for the manner in which they won their advancement. In this way Mdlle. de Querouailles, a beautiful French lady, came to London on a special mission of Louis XIV, and was adopted by our grateful country and sovereign, and figured as Duchess of Portsmouth. In this way the beautiful Aurora of Königsmarck travelling about found favour in the eyes of Augustus of Saxony, and became the mother of Marshal Saxe, who gave us a beating at Fontenoy; and in this manner the lovely sisters Elizabeth and Melusina of Meissenbach (who had actually been driven out of Paris, whither they had travelled on a like errand, by the wise jealousy of the female favourite there in possession) journeyed to Hanover, and became favourites of the serene house there reigning.

That beautiful Aurora von Königsmarck and her brother are wonderful as types of bygone manners, and strange illustrations of the morals of old days. The Königsmarcks were descended from an ancient noble family of Brandenburgh, a branch of which passed into Sweden, where it enriched itself and produced several mighty men of valour.

The founder of the race was Hans Christof, a famous warrior and plunderer of the Thirty Years' War. One of Hans's sons, Otto, appeared as ambassador at the Court of Louis XIV, and had to make a Swedish speech at his reception before the Most Christian King. Otto was a famous dandy and warrior, but he forgot the speech, and what do you think he did? Far from being disconcerted, he recited a portion of the Swedish Catechism to His Most Christian Majesty and his Court, not one of whom understood his lingo with the exception of his own suite, who had to keep their gravity as best they might.

Otto's nephew, Aurora's elder brother, Carl Johann of Königsmarck, a favourite of Charles II, a beauty, a dandy, a warrior, a rascal of more than ordinary mark, escaped but deserved being hanged in England, for the murder of Tom Thynne of Longleat. He had a little brother in London with him at this time,—as great a beauty, as great a dandy, as great a villain as his elder. This lad, Philip of Königsmarck, also was implicated in the affair; and perhaps it is a pity he ever brought his pretty neck out of it. He went over to Hanover, and was soon appointed colonel of a regiment of H. E. Highness's dragoons. In early life he had been page in the Court of Celle; and it was said that he and the pretty Princess Sophia Dorothea, who by this time was married to her cousin George the Electoral prince, had been in love with each other as children. Their loves were now to be renewed, not innocently, and to come to a fearful end.

A biography of the wife of George I, by Dr. Doran, has lately appeared, and I confess I am astounded at the verdict which that writer has delivered, and at his acquittal of this most unfortunate lady. That she had a cold selfish libertine of a husband no one can doubt; but that the bad husband had a bad wife is equally clear. She was married to her cousin for money or convenience, as all princesses were married. She was most beautiful, lively, witty, accomplished: his brutality outraged her: his silence and coldness chilled her: his cruelty insulted her. No wonder she did not love him. How could love be a part of the compact in such a marriage as that? With this unlucky heart to dispose of, the poor creature bestowed it on Philip of Königsmarck, than whom a greater scamp does not walk the history of the seventeenth century. A hundred and eighty years after the fellow was thrust into his unknown grave, a Swedish professor lights upon a box of letters in the University Library at Upsala, written by Philip and Dorothea to each other, and telling their miserable story.

The bewitching Königsmarck had conquered two female hearts in Hanover. Besides the Electoral prince's lovely young wife Sophia Dorothea, Philip had inspired a passion in a hideous old Court lady, the Countess of Platen. The princess seems to have pursued him with the fidelity of many years. Heaps of letters followed him on his campaigns, and were answered by the daring adventurer. The princess wanted to fly with him; to quit her odious husband at any rate. She besought her parents to receive her back; had a notion of taking refuge in France and going over to the Catholic religion; had absolutely packed her jewels for flight, and very likely arranged its details with her lover, in that last long night's interview, after which Philip of Königsmarck was seen no more.

Königsmarck, inflamed with drink—there is scarcely any vice of which, according to his own showing, this gentleman was not a practitioner—had boasted at a supper at Dresden of his intimacy with the two Hanoverian ladies, not only with the princess, but with another lady powerful in Hanover. The Countess Platen, the old favourite of the Elector, hated the young Electoral princess. The young lady had a lively wit, and constantly made fun of the old one. The princess's jokes were conveyed to the old Platen just as our idle words are carried about at this present day: and so they both hated each other.

The characters in the tragedy, of which the curtain was now about to fall, are about as dark a set as eye ever rested on. There is the jolly prince, shrewd, selfish, scheming, loving his cups and his ease (I think his good humour makes the tragedy but darker); his princess, who speaks little but observes all; his old, painted Jezebel of a mistress; his son, the Electoral prince, shrewd too, quiet, selfish, not ill-humoured, and generally silent, except when goaded into fury by the intolerable tongue of his lovely wife; there is poor Sophia Dorothea, with her coquetry and her wrongs, and her passionate attachment to her scamp of a lover, and her wild imprudences, and her mad artifices, and her insane fidelity, and her furious jealousy regarding her husband (though she loathed and cheated him), and her prodigious falsehoods; and the confidante, of course, into whose hands the letters are slipped; and there is Lothario, finally, than whom, as I have said, one can't imagine a more handsome, wicked, worthless reprobate.

How that perverse fidelity of passion pursues the villain! How madly true the woman is, and how astoundingly she lies! She has bewitched two or three persons who have taken her up, and they won't believe in her wrong. Like Mary of Scotland, she finds adherents ready to conspire for her even in history, and people who have to deal with her are charmed, and fascinated, and bedevilled. How devotedly Miss Strickland has stood by Mary's innocence! Are there not scores of ladies in this audience who persist in it too? Innocent! I remember as a boy how a great party persisted in declaring Caroline of Brunswick was a martyred angel. So was Helen of Greece innocent. She never ran away with Paris, the dangerous young Trojan. Menelaus, her husband, ill-used her, and there never was any siege of Troy at all. So was Bluebeard's wife innocent. She never peeped into the closet where the other wives were with their heads off. She never dropped the key, or stained it with blood; and her brothers were quite right in finishing Bluebeard, the cowardly brute! Yes, Caroline of Brunswick was innocent: and Madame Laffarge never poisoned her husband; and Mary of Scotland never blew up hers; and poor Sophia Dorothea was never unfaithful; and Eve never took the apple—it was a cowardly fabrication of the serpent's.

George Louis has been held up to execration as a murderous Bluebeard, whereas the Electoral prince had no share in the transaction in which Philip of Königsmarck was scuffled out of this mortal scene. The prince was absent when the catastrophe came. The princess had had a hundred warnings; mild hints from her husband's parents; grim remonstrances from himself—but took no more heed of this advice than such besotted poor wretches do. On the night of Sunday, the 1st of July, 1694, Königsmarck paid a long visit to the princess, and left her to get ready for flight. Her husband was away at Berlin; her carriages and horses were prepared and ready for the elopement. Meanwhile, the spies of Countess Platen had brought the news to their mistress. She went to Ernest Augustus, and procured from the Elector an order for the arrest of the Swede. On the way by which he was to come, four guards were commissioned to take him. He strove to cut his way through the four men, and wounded more than one of them. They fell upon him; cut him down; and, as he was lying wounded on the ground, the countess, his enemy, whom he had betrayed and insulted, came out and beheld him prostrate. He cursed her with his dying lips, and the furious woman stamped upon his mouth with her heel. He was dispatched presently; his body burnt the next day; and all traces of the man disappeared. The guards who killed him were enjoined silence under severe penalties. The princess was reported to be ill in her apartments, from which she was taken in October of the same year, being then eight-and-twenty years old, and consigned to the castle of Ahlden, where she remained a prisoner for no less than thirty-two years. A separation had been pronounced previously between her and her husband. She was called henceforth the "Princess of Ahlden", and her silent husband no more uttered her name.

Four years after the Königsmarck catastrophe, Ernest Augustus, the first Elector of Hanover, died, and George Louis, his son, reigned in his stead. Sixteen years he reigned in Hanover, after which he became, as we know, King of Great Britain, France, and Ireland, Defender of the Faith. The wicked old Countess Platen died in the year 1706. She had lost her sight, but nevertheless the legend says that she constantly saw Königsmarck's ghost by her wicked old bed. And so there was an end of her.

In the year 1700, the little Duke of Gloucester, the last of poor Queen Anne's children, died, and the folks of Hanover straightway became of prodigious importance in England. The Electress Sophia was declared the next in succession to the English throne. George Louis was created Duke of Cambridge; grand deputations were sent over from our country to Deutschland; but Queen Anne, whose weak heart hankered after her relatives at St. Germains, never could be got to allow her cousin, the Elector Duke of Cambridge, to come and pay his respects to her Majesty, and take his seat in her House of Peers. Had the queen lasted a month longer; had the English Tories been as bold and resolute as they were clever and crafty; had the prince whom the nation loved and pitied been equal to his fortune, George Louis had never talked German in St. James's Chapel Royal.

When the crown did come to George Louis he was in no hurry about putting it on. He waited at home for awhile; took an affecting farewell of his dear Hanover and Herrenhausen; and set out in the most leisurely manner to ascend "the throne of his ancestors", as he called it in his first speech to Parliament. He brought with him a compact body of Germans, whose society he loved, and whom he kept round the royal person. He had his faithful German chamberlains; his German secretaries; his negroes, captives of his bow and spear in Turkish wars; his two ugly, elderly German favourites, Mesdames of Kielmansegge and Schulenberg, whom he created respectively Countess of Darlington and Duchess of Kendal. The duchess was tall, and lean of stature, and hence was irreverently nicknamed the Maypole. The countess was a large-sized noblewoman, and this elevated personage was denominated the Elephant. Both of these ladies loved Hanover and its delights; clung round the linden-trees of the great Herrenhausen avenue, and at first would not quit the place. Schulenberg, in fact, could not come on account of her debts; but finding the Maypole would not come, the Elephant packed up her trunk and slipped out of Hanover unwieldy as she was. On this the Maypole straightway put herself in motion, and followed her beloved George Louis. One seems to be speaking of Captain Macheath, and Polly, and Lucy. The king we had selected; the courtiers who came in his train; the English nobles who came to welcome him, and on many of whom the shrewd old cynic turned his back—I protest it is a wonderful satirical picture. I am a citizen waiting at Greenwich pier, say, and crying hurrah for King George; and yet I can scarcely keep my countenance, and help laughing at the enormous absurdity of this advent!

Here we are, all on our knees. Here is the Archbishop of Canterbury prostrating himself to the head of his Church, with Kielmansegge and Schulenberg with their raddled cheeks grinning behind the Defender of the Faith. Here is my Lord Duke of Marlborough kneeling too, the greatest warrior of all times; he who betrayed King William—betrayed King James II—betrayed Queen Anne—betrayed England to the French, the Elector to the Pretender, the Pretender to the Elector; and here are my Lords Oxford and Bolingbroke, the latter of whom has just tripped up the heels of the former; and if a month's more time had been allowed him, would have had King James at Westminster. The great Whig gentlemen made their bows and congees with proper decorum and ceremony; but yonder keen old schemer knows the value of their loyalty. "Loyalty," he must think, "as applied to me—it is absurd! There are fifty nearer heirs to the throne than I am. I am but an accident, and you fine Whig gentlemen take me for your own sake, not for mine. You Tories hate me; you archbishop, smirking on your knees, and prating about Heaven, you know I don't care a fig for your Thirty-nine Articles, and can't understand a word of your stupid sermons. You, my Lords Bolingbroke and Oxford—you know you were conspiring against me a month ago; and you, my Lord Duke of Marlborough—you would sell me or any man else, if you found your advantage in it. Come, my good Melusina, come, my honest Sophia, let us go into my private room, and have some oysters and some Rhine wine, and some pipes afterwards: let us make the best of our situation; let us take what we can get, and leave these bawling, brawling, lying English to shout, and fight, and cheat, in their own way!"

If Swift had not been committed to the statesmen of the losing side, what a fine satirical picture we might have had of that general sauve qui peut amongst the Tory party! How mum the Tories became; how the House of Lords and House of Commons chopped round; and how decorously the majorities welcomed King George!

Bolingbroke, making his last speech in the House of Lords, pointed out the shame of peerage, where several lords concurred to condemn in one general vote all that they had approved in former

Parliaments by many particular resolutions. And so their conduct was shameful. St. John had the best of the argument, but the worst of the vote. Bad times were come for him. He talked philosophy, and professed innocence. He courted retirement, and was ready to meet persecution; but, hearing that honest Mat Prior, who had been recalled from Paris, was about to peach regarding the past transactions, the philosopher bolted, and took that magnificent head of his out of the ugly reach of the axe. Oxford, the lazy and good-humoured, had more courage, and awaited the storm at home. He and Mat Prior both had lodgings in the Tower, and both brought their heads safe out of that dangerous menagerie. When Atterbury was carried off to the same den a few years afterwards, and it was asked, what next should be done with him? "Done with him? Fling him to the lions," Cadogan said, Marlborough's lieutenant. But the British lion of those days did not care much for drinking the blood of peaceful peers and poets, or crunching the bones of bishops. Only four men were executed in London for the rebellion of 1715; and twenty-two in Lancashire. Above a thousand taken in arms, submitted to the king's mercy, and petitioned to be transported to his Majesty's colonies in America. I have heard that their descendants took the loyalist side in the disputes which arose sixty years after. It is pleasant to find that a friend of ours, worthy Dick Steele, was for letting off the rebels with their lives.

As one thinks of what might have been, how amusing the speculation is! We know how the doomed Scottish gentlemen came out at Lord Mar's summons, mounted the white cockade, that has been a flower of sad poetry ever since, and rallied round the ill-omened Stuart standard at Braemar. Mar, with 8,000 men, and but 1,500 opposed to him, might have driven the enemy over the Tweed, and taken possession of the whole of Scotland; but that the Pretender's duke did not venture to move when the day was his own. Edinburgh Castle might have been in King James's hands; but that the men who were to escalade it stayed to drink his health at the tavern, and arrived two hours too late at the rendezvous under the castle wall. There was sympathy enough in the town—the projected attack seems to have been known there—Lord Mahon quotes Sinclair's account of a gentleman not concerned, who told Sinclair, that he was in a house that evening where eighteen of them were drinking, as the facetious landlady said, "powdering their hair," for the attack of the castle. Suppose they had not stopped to powder their hair? Edinburgh Castle, and town, and all Scotland were King James's. The north of England rises, and marches over Barnet Heath upon London. Wyndham is up in Somersetshire; Packington in Worcestershire; and Vivian in Cornwall. The Elector of Hanover, and his hideous mistresses, pack up the plate, and perhaps the crown jewels in London, and are off via Harwich and Helvoetsluys, for dear old Deutschland. The king—God save him!—lands at Dover, with tumultuous applause; shouting multitudes, roaring cannon, the Duke of Marlborough weeping tears of joy, and all the bishops kneeling in the mud. In a few years, mass is said in St. Paul's; matins and vespers are sung in York Minster; and Dr. Swift is turned out of his stall and deanery house at St. Patrick's, to give place to Father Dominic, from Salamanca. All these changes were possible then, and once thirty years afterwards—all this we might have had, but for the pulveris exigui jactu, that little toss of powder for the hair which the Scotch conspirators stopped to take at the tavern.

You understand the distinction I would draw between history—of which I do not aspire to be an expounder—and manners and life such as these sketches would describe. The rebellion breaks out in the north; its story is before you in a hundred volumes, in none more fairly than in the excellent narrative of Lord Mahon, The clans are up in Scotland; Derwentwater, Nithsdale and Forster are in arms in Northumberland—these are matters of history, for which you are referred to the due chroniclers. The Guards are set to watch the streets, and prevent the people wearing white roses. I read presently of a couple of soldiers almost flogged to death for wearing oak boughs in their hats on the 29th of May— another badge of the beloved Stuarts. It is with these we have to do, rather than the marches and battles of the armies to which the poor fellows belonged—with statesmen, and how they looked, and how they lived, rather than with measures of state, which belong to history alone. For example, at the close of the old queen's reign, it is known the Duke of Marlborough left the kingdom—after what menaces, after what prayers, lies, bribes offered, taken, refused, accepted; after what dark doubling and tacking, let history, if she can or dare, say. The queen dead; who so eager to return as my lord duke? Who shouts God save the king! so lustily as the great conqueror of Blenheim and Malplaquet? (By the way, he will send over some more money for the Pretender yet, on the sly.) Who lays his hand on his blue ribbon, and lifts his eyes more gracefully to heaven than this hero? He makes a quasi-triumphal entrance into London, by Temple Bar, in his enormous gilt coach—and the enormous gilt coach breaks down somewhere by Chancery Lane, and his highness is obliged to get another. There it is we have him. We are with the mob in the crowd, not with the great folks in the procession. We are not the Historic Muse, but her ladyship's attendant, tale-bearer—valet de chambre—for whom no man is a hero; and, as yonder one steps from his carriage to the next handy conveyance, we take the number of the hack; we look all over at his stars, ribbons, embroidery; we think within ourselves, O you unfathomable schemer! O you warrior invincible! O you beautiful smiling Judas! What master would you not kiss or betray? What traitor's head, blackening on the spikes on yonder gate, ever hatched a tithe of the treason which has worked under your periwig?

We have brought our Georges to London city, and if we would behold its aspect, may see it in Hogarth's lively perspective of Cheapside, or read of it in a hundred contemporary books which paint the manners of that age. Our dear old Spectator looks smiling upon the streets, with their innumerable signs, and describes them with his charming humour. "Our streets are filled with 'Blue Boars', 'Black Swans', and 'Red Lions', not to mention 'Flying Pigs' and 'Hogs in Armour', with other creatures more extraordinary than any in the deserts of Africa." A few of these quaint old figures still remain in London town. You may still see there, and over its old hostel in Ludgate Hill, the "Belle Sauvage" to whom the Spectator so pleasantly alludes in that paper; and who was, probably, no other than the sweet American Pocahontas, who rescued from death the daring Captain Smith. There is the "Lion's Head'" down whose jaws the Spectator's own letters were passed; and over a great banker's in Fleet Street, the effigy of the wallet, which the founder of the firm bore when he came into London a country boy. People this street, so ornamented with crowds of swinging chairmen, with servants bawling to clear the way, with Mr. Dean in his cassock, his lackey marching before him; or Mrs. Dinah in her sack, tripping to chapel, her footboy carrying her ladyship's great Prayer-book; with itinerant tradesmen, singing their hundred cries (I remember forty years ago, as a boy in London city, a score of cheery, familiar cries that are silent now). Fancy the beaux thronging to the chocolate-houses, tapping their snuff-boxes as they issue thence, their periwigs appearing over the red curtains. Fancy Saccharissa beckoning and smiling from the upper windows, and a crowd of soldiers brawling and bustling at the door—gentlemen of the Life Guards, clad in scarlet, with blue facings, and laced with gold at the seams; gentlemen of the Horse Grenadiers, in their caps of sky-blue cloth, with the garter embroidered on the front in gold and silver; men of the Halberdiers, in their long red coats, as bluff Harry left them, with their ruffs and velvet flat caps. Perhaps the king's Majesty himself is going to St. James's as we pass. If he is going to Parliament, he is in his coach-and-eight, surrounded by his guards and the high officers of his crown. Otherwise his Majesty only uses a chair, with six footmen walking before, and six yeomen of the guard at the sides of the sedan. The officers in waiting follow the king in coaches. It must be rather slow work.

Our Spectator and Tatler are full of delightful glimpses of the town life of those days. In the company of that charming guide, we may go to the opera, the comedy, the puppet show, the auction, even the cockpit: we can take boat at Temple Stairs, and accompany Sir Roger de Coverley and Mr. Spectator to Spring Garden—it will be called Vauxhall a few years since, when Hogarth will paint for it. Would you not like to step back into the past, and be introduced to Mr. Addison?—not the Right Honourable Joseph

Addison, Esq., George I's Secretary of State, but to the delightful painter of contemporary manners; the man who, when in good humour himself, was the pleasantest companion in all England. I should like to go into Lockit's with him, and drink a bowl along with Sir R. Steele (who has just been knighted by King George, and who does not happen to have any money to pay his share of the reckoning). I should not care to follow Mr. Addison to his secretary's office in Whitehall. There we get into politics. Our business is pleasure, and the town, and the coffee-house, and the theatre, and the Mall. Delightful Spectator! kind friend of leisure hours! happy companion! true Christian gentleman! How much greater, better, you are than the king Mr. Secretary kneels to!

You can have foreign testimony about old-world London, if you like; and my before-quoted friend, Charles Louis, Baron de Pöllnitz, will conduct us to it. "A man of sense," says he, "or a fine gentleman, is never at a loss for company in London, and this is the way the latter passes his time. He rises late, puts on a frock, and, leaving his sword at home, takes his cane, and goes where he pleases. The Park is commonly the place where he walks, because 'tis the Exchange for men of quality. 'Tis the same thing as the Tuileries at Paris, only the Park has a certain beauty of simplicity which cannot be described. The grand walk is called the Mall; is full of people at every hour of the day, but especially at morning and evening, when their Majesties often walk with the royal family, who are attended only by a half-dozen yeomen of the guard, and permit all persons to walk at the same time with them. The ladies and gentlemen always appear in rich dresses, for the English, who, twenty years ago, did not wear gold lace but in their army, are now embroidered and bedaubed as much as the French. I speak of persons of quality; for the citizen still contents himself with a suit of fine cloth, a good hat and wig, and fine linen. Everybody is well clothed here, and even the beggars don't make so ragged an appearance as they do elsewhere." After our friend, the man of quality, has had his morning or undress walk in the Mall, he goes home to dress, and then saunters to some coffee-house or chocolate-house frequented by the persons he would see. "For 'tis a rule with the English to go once a day at least to houses of this sort, where they talk of business and news, read the papers, and often look at one another without opening their lips. And 'tis very well they are so mute: for were they all as talkative as people of other nations, the coffee-houses would be intolerable, and there would be no hearing what one man said where they are so many. The chocolate-house in St. James's Street, where I go every morning to pass away the time, is always so full that a man can scarce turn about in it."

Delightful as London city was, King George I liked to be out of it as much as ever he could; and when there, passed all his time with his Germans. It was with them as with Blücher 100 years afterwards, when the bold old Reiter looked down from St. Paul's, and sighed out, "Was für Plunder!" The German women plundered; the German secretaries plundered; the German cooks and intendants plundered; even Mustapha and Mahomet, the German negroes, had a share of the booty. Take what you can get, was the old monarch's maxim. He was not a lofty monarch, certainly: he was not a patron of the fine arts: but he was not a hypocrite, he was not revengeful, he was not extravagant. Though a despot in Hanover, he was a moderate ruler in England. His aim was to leave it to itself as much as possible, and to live out of it as much as he could. His heart was in Hanover. When taken ill on his last journey, as he was passing through Holland, he thrust his livid head out of the coach-window, and gasped out, "Osnaburg, Osnaburg!" He was more than fifty years of age when he came amongst us: we took him because we wanted him, because he served our turn; we laughed at his uncouth German ways, and sneered at him. He took our loyalty for what it was worth; laid hands on what money he could; kept us assuredly from Popery and wooden shoes. I, for one, would have been on his side in those days. Cynical, and selfish, as he was, he was better than a king out of St. Germains with the French king's orders in his pocket, and a swarm of Jesuits in his train.

The Fates are supposed to interest themselves about royal personages; and so this one had omens and prophecies specially regarding him. He was said to be much disturbed at a prophecy that he should die very soon after his wife; and sure enough, pallid Death, having seized upon the luckless princess in her castle of Ahlden, presently pounced upon H.M. King George I, in his travelling chariot, on the Hanover road. What postilion can outride that pale horseman? It is said, George promised one of his left-handed widows to come to her after death, if leave were granted to him to revisit the glimpses of the moon; and soon after his demise, a great raven actually flying or hopping in at the Duchess of Kendal's window at Twickenham, she chose to imagine the king's spirit inhabited these plumes, and took special care of her sable visitor. Affecting metempsychosis—funereal royal bird! How pathetic is the idea of the duchess weeping over it! When this chaste addition to our English aristocracy died, all her jewels, her plate, her plunder went over to her relations in Hanover. I wonder whether her heirs took the bird, and whether it is still flapping its wings over Herrenhausen?

The days are over in England of that strange religion of king-worship, when priests flattered princes in the Temple of God; when servility was held to be ennobling duty; when beauty and youth tried eagerly for royal favour; and woman's shame was held to be no dishonour. Mended morals and mended manners in Courts and people, are among the priceless consequences of the freedom which George I came to rescue and secure. He kept his compact with his English subjects; and if he escaped no more than other men and monarchs from the vices of his age, at least we may thank him for preserving and transmitting the liberties of ours. In our free air, royal and humble homes have alike been purified; and Truth, the birthright of high and low among us, which quite fearlessly judges our greatest personages, can only speak of them now in words of respect and regard. There are stains in the portrait of the first George, and traits in it which none of us need admire; but, among the nobler features are justice, courage, moderation—and these we may recognize ere we turn the picture to the wall.

George The Second

On the afternoon of the 14th of June, 1727, two horsemen might have been perceived galloping along the road from Chelsea to Richmond. The foremost, cased in the jackboots of the period, was a broad-faced, jolly-looking, and very corpulent cavalier; but, by the manner in which he urged his horse, you might see that he was a bold as well as a skilful rider. Indeed, no man loved sport better; and in the hunting-fields of Norfolk, no squire rode more boldly after the fox, or cheered Ringwood and Sweettips more lustily, than he who now thundered over the Richmond road.

He speedily reached Richmond Lodge, and asked to see the owner of the mansion. The mistress of the house and her ladies, to whom our friend was admitted, said he could not be introduced to the master, however pressing the business might be. The master was asleep after his dinner; he always slept after his dinner: and woe be to the person who interrupted him! Nevertheless, our stout friend of the jackboots put the affrighted ladies aside, opened the forbidden door of the bedroom, wherein upon the bed lay a little gentleman; and here the eager messenger knelt down in his jackboots.

He on the bed started up, and with many oaths and a strong German accent asked who was there, and who dared to disturb him?

"I am Sir Robert Walpole," said the messenger. The awakened sleeper hated Sir Robert Walpole. "I have the honour to announce to your Majesty that your royal father, King George I, died at Osnaburg, on Saturday last, the 10th inst."

"Dat is one big lie!" roared out his sacred Majesty King George II: but Sir Robert Walpole stated the fact, and from that day until three-and-thirty years after, George, the second of the name, ruled over England.

How the king made away with his father's will under the astonished nose of the Archbishop of Canterbury; how he was a choleric little sovereign; how he shook his fist in the face of his father's courtiers; how he kicked his coat and wig about in his rages, and called everybody thief, liar, rascal, with whom he differed: you will read in all the history books; and how he speedily and shrewdly reconciled himself with the bold minister, whom he had hated during his father's life, and by whom he was served during fifteen years of his own with admirable prudence, fidelity, and success. But for Sir Robert Walpole, we should have had the Pretender back again. But for his obstinate love of peace, we should have had wars, which the nation was not strong enough nor united enough to endure. But for his resolute counsels and good-humoured resistance we might have had German despots attempting a Hanoverian regimen over us: we should have had revolt, commotion, want, and tyrannous misrule, in place of a quarter of a century of peace, freedom, and material prosperity, such as the country never enjoyed, until that corrupter of Parliaments, that dissolute tipsy cynic, that courageous lover of peace and liberty, that great citizen, patriot, and statesman governed it. In religion he was little better than a heathen; cracked ribald jokes at bigwigs and bishops, and laughed at High Church and Low. In private life the old pagan revelled in the lowest pleasures: he passed his Sundays tippling at Richmond; and his holidays bawling after dogs, or boozing at Houghton with boors over beef and punch. He cared for letters no more than his master did: he judged human nature so meanly that one is ashamed to have to own that he was right, and that men could be corrupted by means so base. But, with his hireling House of Commons, he defended liberty for us; with his incredulity he kept Church-craft down. There were parsons at Oxford as double-dealing and dangerous as any priests out of Rome, and he routed them both. He gave Englishmen no conquests, but he gave them peace, and ease, and freedom; the three per cents nearly at par; and wheat at five-and six-and-twenty shillings a quarter.

It was lucky for us that our first Georges were not more high-minded men; especially fortunate that they loved Hanover so much as to leave England to have her own way. Our chief troubles began when we got a king who gloried in the name of Briton, and, being born in the country, proposed to rule it. He was no more fit to govern England than his grandfather and great-grandfather, who did not try. It was righting itself during their occupation. The dangerous, noble old spirit of cavalier loyalty was dying out; the stately old English High Church was emptying itself: the questions dropping, which, on one side and the other;—the side of loyalty, prerogative, church, and king;—the side of right, truth, civil and religious freedom,—had set generations of brave men in arms. By the time when George III came to the throne, the combat between loyalty and liberty was come to an end; and Charles Edward, old, tipsy, and childless, was dying in Italy.

Those who are curious about European Court history of the last age know the memoirs of the Margravine of Bayreuth, and what a Court was that of Berlin, where George II's cousins ruled sovereign. Frederick the Great's father knocked down his sons, daughters, officers of state; he kidnapped big men all Europe over to make grenadiers of; his feasts, his parades, his wine parties, his tobacco parties, are all described. Jonathan Wild the Great in language, pleasures, and behaviour, is scarcely more delicate than this German sovereign. Louis XV, his life, and reign, and doings, are told in a thousand French memoirs. Our George II, at least, was not a worse king than his neighbours. He claimed and took the royal exemption from doing right which sovereigns assumed. A dull little man of low tastes he appears to us in England; yet Hervey tells us that this choleric prince was a great sentimentalist, and that his letters—of which he wrote prodigious quantities—were quite dangerous in their powers of fascination. He kept his sentimentalities for his Germans and his queen. With us English, he never chose to be familiar. He has been accused of avarice, yet he did not give much money, and did not leave much behind him. He did not love the fine arts, but he did not pretend to love them. He was no more a hypocrite about religion than his father. He judged men by a low standard; yet, with such men as were near him, was he wrong in judging as he did? He readily detected lying and flattery, and liars and flatterers were perforce his companions. Had he been more of a dupe he might have been more amiable. A dismal experience made him cynical. No boon was it to him to be clear-sighted, and see only selfishness and flattery round about him. What could Walpole tell him about his Lords and Commons, but that they were all venal? Did not his clergy, his courtiers, bring him the same story? Dealing with men and women in his rude, sceptical way, he comes to doubt about honour, male and female, about patriotism, about religion. "He is wild, but he fights like a man," George I, the taciturn, said of his son and successor. Courage George II certainly had. The Electoral Prince, at the head of his father's contingent, had approved himself a good and brave soldier under Eugene and Marlborough. At Oudenarde he specially distinguished himself. At Malplaquet the other claimant to the English throne won but little honour. There was always a question about James's courage. Neither then in Flanders, nor afterwards in his own ancient kingdom of Scotland, did the luckless Pretender show much resolution. But dapper little George had a famous tough spirit of his own, and fought like a Trojan. He called out his brother of Prussia, with sword and pistol; and I wish, for the interest of romancers in general, that that famous duel could have taken place. The two sovereigns hated each other with all their might; their seconds were appointed; the place of meeting was settled; and the duel was only prevented by strong representations made to the two, of the European laughter which would have been caused by such a transaction.

Whenever we hear of dapper George at war, it is certain that he demeaned himself like a little man of valour. At Dettingen his horse ran away with him, and with difficulty was stopped from carrying him into the enemy's lines. The king, dismounting from the fiery quadruped, said bravely: "Now I know I shall not run away;" and placed himself at the head of the foot, drew his sword, brandishing it at the whole of the French army, and calling out to his own men to come on, in bad English, but with the most famous pluck and spirit. In '45, when the Pretender was at Derby, and many people began to look pale, the king never lost his courage—not he. "Pooh! don't talk to me that stuff!" he said, like a gallant little prince as he was, and never for one moment allowed his equanimity, or his business, or his pleasures, or his travels, to be disturbed. On public festivals he always appeared in the hat and coat he wore on the famous day of Oudenarde; and the people laughed, but kindly, at the odd old garment, for bravery never goes out of fashion.

In private life the prince showed himself a worthy descendant of his father. In this respect, so much has been said about the first George's manners, that we need not enter into a description of the son's German harem. In 1705 he married a princess remarkable for beauty, for cleverness, for learning, for good temper—one of the truest and fondest wives ever prince was blessed with, and who loved him and was faithful to him, and he, in his coarse fashion, loved her to the last. It must be told to the honour of Caroline of Anspach, that, at the time when German princes thought no more of changing their religion than you of altering your cap, she refused to give up Protestantism for the other creed, although an Archduke, afterwards to be an Emperor, was offered to her for a bridegroom. Her Protestant relations in Berlin were angry at her rebellious spirit; it was they who tried to convert her (it is droll to think that Frederick the Great, who had no religion at all, was known for a long time in England as the Protestant hero), and these good Protestants set upon Caroline a certain Father Urban, a very skilful Jesuit, and famous winner of souls. But she routed the Jesuit; and she refused Charles VI; and she married the little Electoral Prince of Hanover, whom she tended with love, and with every manner of sacrifice, with artful kindness, with tender flattery, with entire self-devotion, thenceforward until her life's end.

When George I made his first visit to Hanover, his son was appointed regent during the royal absence. But this honour was never again conferred on the Prince of Wales; he and his father fell out presently. On the occasion of the christening of his second son, a royal row took place, and the prince, shaking his fist in the Duke of Newcastle's face, called him a rogue, and provoked his august father. He and his wife were turned out of St. James's, and their princely children taken from them, by order of the royal head of the family. Father and mother wept piteously at parting from their little ones. The young ones sent some cherries, with their love, to papa and mamma; the parents watered the fruit with tears. They had no tears thirty-five years afterwards, when Prince Frederick died—their eldest son, their heir, their enemy.

The king called his daughter-in-law "cette diablesse madame la princesse". The frequenters of the latter's Court were forbidden to appear at the king's: their royal highnesses going to Bath, we read how the courtiers followed them thither, and paid that homage in Somersetshire which was forbidden in London. That phrase of "cette diablesse madame la princesse" explains one cause of the wrath of her royal papa. She was a very clever woman: she had a keen sense of humour: she had a dreadful tongue: she turned into ridicule the antiquated sultan and his hideous harem. She wrote savage letters about him home to members of her family. So, driven out from the royal presence, the prince and princess set up for themselves in Leicester Fields, "where," says Walpole, "the most promising of the young gentlemen of the next party, and the prettiest and liveliest of the young ladies, formed the new Court." Besides Leicester House, they had their lodge at Richmond, frequented by some of the pleasantest company of those days. There were the Herveys, and Chesterfield, and little Mr. Pope from Twickenham, and with him, sometimes, the savage Dean of St. Patrick's, and quite a bevy of young ladies, whose pretty faces smile on us out of history. There was Lepell, famous in ballad song; and the saucy, charming Mary Bellenden, who would have none of the Prince of Wales's fine compliments, who folded her arms across her breast, and bade H.R.H. keep off; and knocked his purse of guineas into his face, and told him she was tired of seeing him count them. He was not an august monarch, this Augustus. Walpole tells how, one night at the royal card-table, the playful princesses pulled a chair away from under Lady Deloraine, who, in revenge, pulled the king's from under him, so that his Majesty fell on the carpet. In whatever posture one sees this royal George, he is ludicrous somehow; even at Dettingen, where he fought so bravely, his figure is absurd—calling out in his broken English, and lunging with his rapier, like a fencing-master. In contemporary caricatures, George's son, "the Hero of Culloden," is also made an object of considerable fun, as witness the following picture of him defeated by the French (1757) at Hastenbeck:

I refrain to quote from Walpole regarding George—for those charming volumes are in the hands of all who love the gossip of the last century. Nothing can be more cheery than Horace's letters. Fiddles sing all through them: wax-lights, fine dresses, fine jokes, fine plate, fine equipages, glitter and sparkle there: never was such a brilliant, jigging, smirking Vanity Fair as that through which he leads us. Hervey, the next great authority, is a darker spirit. About him there is something frightful: a few years since his heirs opened the lid of the Ickworth box; it was as if a Pompeii was opened to us—the last century dug up, with its temples and its games, its chariots, its public places—lupanaria. Wandering through that city of the dead, that dreadfully selfish time, through those godless intrigues and feasts, through those crowds, pushing, and eager, and struggling—rouged, and lying, and fawning—I have wanted some one to be friends with. I have said to friends conversant with that history, Show me some good person about that Court; find me, among those selfish courtiers, those dissolute, gay people, some one being that I can love and regard. There is that strutting little sultan, George II; there is that hunchbacked, beetle-browed Lord Chesterfield; there is John Hervey, with his deadly smile, and ghastly, painted face—I hate them. There is Hoadly, cringing from one bishopric to another: yonder comes little Mr. Pope, from Twickenham, with his friend, the Irish dean, in his new cassock, bowing too, but with rage flashing from under his bushy eyebrows, and scorn and hate quivering in his smile. Can you be fond of these? Of Pope I might: at least I might love his genius, his wit, his greatness, his sensibility—with a certain conviction that at some fancied slight, some sneer which he imagined, he would turn upon me and stab me. Can you trust the queen? She is not of our order: their very position makes kings and queens lonely. One inscrutable attachment that inscrutable woman has. To that she is faithful, through all trial, neglect, pain, and time. Save her husband, she really cares for no created being. She is good enough to her children, and even fond enough of them: but she would chop them all up into little pieces to please him. In her intercourse with all around her, she was perfectly kind, gracious, and natural; but friends may die, daughters may depart, she will be as perfectly kind and gracious to the next set. If the king wants her, she will smile upon him, be she ever so sad; and walk with him, be she ever so weary; and laugh at his brutal jokes, be she in ever so much pain of body or heart. Caroline's devotion to her husband is a prodigy to read of. What charm had the little man? What was there in those wonderful letters of thirty pages long, which he wrote to her when he was absent, and to his mistresses at Hanover, when he was in London with his wife? Why did Caroline, the most lovely and accomplished princess of Germany, take a little red-faced staring princeling for a husband, and refuse an emperor? Why, to her last hour, did she love him so? She killed herself because she loved him so. She had the gout, and would plunge her feet in cold water in order to walk with him. With the film of death over her eyes, writhing in intolerable pain, she yet had a livid smile and a gentle word for her master. You have read the wonderful history of that death-bed? How she bade him marry again, and the reply the old king blubbered out, "Non, non: j'aurai des maitresses." There never was such a ghastly farce. I watch the astonishing scene—I stand by that awful bedside, wondering at the ways in which God has ordained the lives, loves, rewards, successes, passions, actions, ends of his creatures—and can't but laugh, in the presence of death, and with the saddest heart. In that often-quoted passage from Lord Hervey, in which the queen's death-bed is described, the grotesque horror of the details surpasses all satire: the dreadful humour of the scene is more terrible than Swift's blackest pages, or Fielding's fiercest irony. The man who wrote the story had something diabolical about him: the terrible verses which Pope wrote respecting Hervey, in one of his own moods of almost fiendish malignity, I fear are true. I am frightened as I look back into the past, and fancy I behold that ghastly, beautiful face; as I think of the queen writhing on her death-bed, and crying out, "Pray!—pray!"—of the royal old sinner by her side, who kisses her dead lips with frantic grief, and leaves her to sin more;—of the bevy of courtly clergymen, and the archbishop, whose prayers she rejects, and who are obliged for propriety's sake to shuffle off the anxious inquiries of the public, and vow that her Majesty quitted this life "in a heavenly frame of mind". What a life!—to what ends devoted! What a vanity of vanities! It is a theme for another pulpit than the lecturer's. For a pulpit?—I think the part which pulpits play in the deaths of kings is the most ghastly of all the ceremonial: the lying eulogies, the blinking of disagreeable truths, the sickening flatteries, the simulated grief, the falsehood and sycophancies—all uttered in the name of Heaven in our State churches: these monstrous threnodies have been sung from time immemorial over kings and queens, good, bad, wicked, licentious. The State parson must bring out his commonplaces; his apparatus of rhetorical black-hangings. Dead king or live king, the clergyman must flatter him—announce his piety whilst living, and when dead, perform the obsequies of "our most religious and gracious king".

I read that Lady Yarmouth (my most religious and gracious king's favourite) sold a bishopric to a clergyman for 5,000 l. (She betted him 5,000 l. that he would not be made a bishop, and he lost, and paid her.) Was he the only prelate of his time led up by such hands for consecration? As I peep into George II's St. James's, I see crowds of cassocks rustling up the back-stairs of the ladies of the Court; stealthy clergy slipping purses into their laps; that godless old king yawning under his canopy in his Chapel Royal, as the chaplain before him is discoursing. Discoursing about what?—about righteousness and judgement? Whilst the chaplain is preaching, the king is chattering in German almost as loud as the preacher; so loud that the clergyman—it may be one Dr. Young, he who wrote Night Thoughts, and discoursed on the splendours of the stars, the glories of heaven, and utter vanities of this world— actually burst out crying in his pulpit because the Defender of the Faith and dispenser of bishoprics would not listen to him! No wonder that the clergy were corrupt and indifferent amidst this indifference and corruption. No wonder that sceptics multiplied and morals degenerated, so far as they depended on the influence of such a king. No wonder that Whitfield cried out in the wilderness, that Wesley quitted the insulted temple to pray on the hillside. I look with reverence on those men at that time. Which is the sublimer spectacle—the good John Wesley, surrounded by his congregation of miners at the pit's mouth, or the queen's chaplains mumbling through their morning office in their ante-room, under the picture of the great Venus, with the door opened into the adjoining chamber, where the queen is dressing, talking scandal to Lord Hervey, or uttering sneers at Lady Suffolk, who is kneeling with the basin at her mistress's side? I say I am scared as I look round at this society—at this king, at these courtiers, at these politicians, at these bishops—at this flaunting vice and levity. Whereabouts in this Court is the honest man? Where is the pure person one may like? The air stifles one with its sickly perfumes. There are some old-world follies and some absurd ceremonials about our Court of the present day, which I laugh at, but as an Englishman, contrasting it with the past, shall I not acknowledge the change of to-day? As the mistress of St. James's passes me now, I salute the sovereign, wise, moderate, exemplary of life; the good mother; the good wife; the accomplished lady; the enlightened friend of art; the tender sympathizer in her people's glories and sorrows.

Of all the Court of George and Caroline, I find no one but Lady Suffolk with whom it seems pleasant and kindly to hold converse. Even the misogynist Croker, who edited her letters, loves her, and has that regard for her with which her sweet graciousness seems to have inspired almost all men and some women who came near her. I have noted many little traits which go to prove the charms of her character (it is not merely because she is charming, but because she is characteristic, that I allude to her). She writes delightfully sober letters. Addressing Mr. Gay at Tunbridge (he was, you know, a poet, penniless and in disgrace), she says: "The place you are in, has strangely filled your head with physicians and cures; but, take my word for it, many a fine lady has gone there to drink the waters without being sick; and many a man has complained of the loss of his heart, who had it in his own possession. I desire you will keep yours; for I shall not be very fond of a friend without one, and I have a great mind you should be in the number of mine."

When Lord Peterborough was seventy years old, that indomitable youth addressed some flaming love—, or rather gallantry—, letters to Mrs. Howard—curious relics they are of the romantic manner of wooing sometimes in use in those days. It is not passion; it is not love; it is gallantry: a mixture of earnest and acting; high-flown compliments, profound bows, vows, sighs, and ogles, in the manner of the Clelie romances, and Millamont and Doricourt in the comedy. There was a vast elaboration of ceremonies and etiquette, of raptures—a regulated form for kneeling and wooing which has quite passed out of our downright manners. Henrietta Howard accepted the noble old earl's philandering; answered the queer love-letters with due acknowledgement; made a profound curtsey to Peterborough's profound bow; and got John Gay to help her in the composition of her letters in reply to her old knight. He wrote her charming verses, in which there was truth as well as grace. "O wonderful creature!" he writes:—

O wonderful creature, a woman of reason!
Never grave out of pride, never gay out of season!
When so easy to guess who this angel should be,
Who would think Mrs. Howard ne'er dreamt it was she?

The great Mr. Pope also celebrated her in lines not less pleasant, and painted a portrait of what must certainly have been a delightful lady:—

I know a thing that's most uncommon—
Envy, be silent and attend!—
I know a reasonable woman,
Handsome, yet witty, and a friend:

Not warp'd by passion, aw'd by rumour,
Not grave through pride, or gay through folly:
An equal mixture of good humour
And exquisite soft melancholy.

Has she no faults, then (Envy says), sir?

Yes, she has one, I must aver—
When all the world conspires to praise her,
The woman's deaf, and does not hear!

Even the women concurred in praising and loving her. The Duchess of Queensberry bears testimony to her amiable qualities, and writes to her: "I tell you so and so, because you love children, and to have children love you." The beautiful, jolly Mary Bellenden, represented by contemporaries as "the most perfect creature ever known", writes very pleasantly to her "dear Howard", her "dear Swiss", from the country, whither Mary had retired after her marriage, and when she gave up being a maid of honour. "How do you do, Mrs. Howard?" Mary breaks out. "How do you do, Mrs. Howard? that is all I have to say. This afternoon I am taken with a fit of writing; but as to matter, I have nothing better to entertain you, than news of my farm. I therefore give you the following list of the stock of eatables that I am fatting for my private tooth. It is well known to the whole county of Kent, that I have four fat calves, two fat hogs, fit for killing, twelve promising black pigs, two young chickens, three fine geese, with thirteen eggs under each (several being duck-eggs, else the others do not come to maturity); all this, with rabbits, and pigeons, and carp in plenty, beef and mutton at reasonable rates. Now, Howard, if you have a mind to stick a knife into anything I have named, say so!"

A jolly set must they have been, those maids of honour. Pope introduces us to a whole bevy of them, in a pleasant letter. "I went," he says, "by water to Hampton Court, and met the Prince, with all his ladies, on horseback, coming from hunting. Mrs. Bellenden and Mrs. Lepell took me into protection, contrary to the laws against harbouring Papists, and gave me a dinner, with something I liked better, an opportunity of conversation with Mrs. Howard. We all agreed that the life of a maid of honour was of all things the most miserable, and wished that all women who envied it had a specimen of it. To eat Westphalia ham of a morning, ride over hedges and ditches on borrowed hacks, come home in the heat of the day with a fever, and (what is worse a hundred times) with a red mark on the forehead from an uneasy hat—all this may qualify them to make excellent wives for hunters. As soon as they wipe off the heat of the day, they must simper an hour and catch cold in the princess's apartment; from thence to dinner with what appetite they may; and after that till midnight, work, walk, or think which way they please. No lone house in Wales, with a mountain and rookery, is more contemplative than this Court. Miss Lepell walked with me three or four hours by moonlight, and we met no creature of any quality but the king, who gave audience to the vice-chamberlain all alone under the garden wall."

I fancy it was a merrier England, that of our ancestors, than the island which we inhabit. People high and low amused themselves very much more. I have calculated the manner in which statesmen and persons of condition passed their time—and what with drinking, and dining, and supping, and cards, wonder how they got through their business at all. They played all sorts of games, which, with the exception of cricket and tennis, have quite gone out of our manners now. In the old prints of St. James's Park, you still see the marks along the walk, to note the balls when the Court played at Mall. Fancy Birdcage Walk now so laid out, and Lord John and Lord Palmerston knocking balls up and down the avenue! Most of those jolly sports belong to the past, and the good old games of England are only to be found in old novels, in old ballads, or the columns of dingy old newspapers, which say how a main of cocks is to be fought at Winchester between the Winchester men and the Hampton men; or how the Cornwall men and the Devon men are going to hold a great wrestling match at Totnes, and so on.

A hundred and twenty years ago there were not only country towns in England, but people who inhabited them. We were very much more gregarious; we were amused by very simple pleasures. Every town had its fair, every village its wake. The old poets have sung a hundred jolly ditties about great cudgel-playings, famous grinning through horse-collars, great maypole meetings, and morris-dances. The girls used to run races clad in very light attire; and the kind gentry and good parsons thought no shame in looking on. Dancing bears went about the country with pipe and tabor. Certain well-known tunes were sung all over the land for hundreds of years, and high and low rejoiced in that simple music. Gentlemen who wished to entertain their female friends constantly sent for a band. When Beau Fielding, a mighty fine gentleman, was courting the lady whom he married, he treated her and her companion at his lodgings to a supper from the tavern, and after supper they sent out for a fiddler—three of them. Fancy the three, in a great wainscoted room, in Covent Garden or Soho, lighted by two or three candles in silver sconces, some grapes and a bottle of Florence wine on the table, and the honest fiddler playing old tunes in quaint old minor keys, as the Beau takes out one lady after the other, and solemnly dances with her!

The very great folks, young noblemen, with their governors, and the like, went abroad and made the great tour; the home satirists jeered at the Frenchified and Italian ways which they brought back; but the greater number of people never left the country. The jolly squire often had never been twenty miles from home. Those who did go went to the baths, to Harrogate, or Scarborough, or Bath, or Epsom. Old letters are full of these places of pleasure. Gay writes to us about the fiddlers at Tunbridge; of the ladies having merry little private balls amongst themselves; and the gentlemen entertaining them by turns with tea and music. One of the young beauties whom he met did not care for tea: "We have a young lady here," he says, "that is very particular in her desires. I have known some young ladies, who, if ever they prayed, would ask for some equipage or title, a husband or matadores: but this lady, who is but seventeen, and has 30,000 l. to her fortune, places all her wishes on a pot of good ale. When her friends, for the sake of her shape and complexion, would dissuade her from it, she answers, with the truest sincerity, that by the loss of shape and complexion she could only lose a husband, whereas ale is her passion."

Every country town had its assembly-room—mouldy old tenements, which we may still see in deserted inn-yards, in decayed provincial cities, out of which the great wen of London has sucked all the life. York, at assize time, and throughout the winter, harboured a large society of northern gentry. Shrewsbury was celebrated for its festivities. At Newmarket, I read of "a vast deal of good company, besides rogues and blacklegs"; at Norwich, of two assemblies, with a prodigious crowd in the hall, the rooms, and the gallery. In Cheshire (it is a maid of honour of Queen Caroline who writes, and who is longing to be back at Hampton Court, and the fun there) I peep into a country house, and see a very merry party: "We meet in the work-room before nine, eat and break a joke or two till twelve, then we repair to our own chambers and make ourselves ready, for it cannot be called dressing. At noon the great bell fetches us into a parlour, adorned with all sorts of fine arms, poisoned darts, several pair of old boots and shoes worn by men of might, with the stirrups of King Charles I, taken from him at Edgehill,"—and there they have their dinner, after which comes dancing and supper.

As for Bath, all history went and bathed and drank there. George II and his queen, Prince Frederick and his Court, scarce a character one can mention of the early last century, but was seen in that famous Pump-room where Beau Nash presided, and his picture hung between the busts of Newton and Pope:

This picture, placed these busts between,
Gives satire all its strength:
Wisdom and Wit are little seen,
But Folly at full length.

I should like to have seen the Folly. It was a splendid, embroidered, be-ruffled, snuff-boxed, red-heeled, impertinent Folly, and knew how to make itself respected. I should like to have seen that noble old madcap Peterborough in his boots (he actually had the audacity to walk about Bath in boots!), with his blue ribbon and stars, and a cabbage under each arm, and a chicken in his hand, which he had been cheapening for his dinner. Chesterfield came there many a time and gambled for hundreds, and grinned through his gout. Mary Wortley was there, young and beautiful; and Mary Wortley, old, hideous, and snuffy. Miss Chudleigh came there, slipping away from one husband, and on the look-out for another. Walpole passed many a day there; sickly, supercilious, absurdly dandified, and affected; with a brilliant wit, a delightful sensibility; and for his friends, a most tender, generous, and faithful heart. And if you and I had been alive then, and strolling down Milsom Street—hush! we should have taken our hats off, as an awful, long, lean, gaunt figure, swathed in flannels, passed by in its chair, and a livid face looked out from the window—great fierce eyes staring from under a bushy, powdered wig, a terrible frown, a terrible Roman nose—and we whisper to one another, "There he is! There's the great commoner! There is Mr. Pitt!" As we walk away, the abbey bells are set a-ringing; and we meet our testy friend Toby Smollett, on the arm of James Quin the actor, who tells us that the bells ring for Mr. Bullock, an eminent cowkeeper from Tottenham, who has just arrived to drink the waters; and Toby shakes his cane at the door of Colonel Ringworm—the Creole gentleman's lodgings next his own—where the colonel's two negroes are practising on the French horn.

When we try to recall social England, we must fancy it playing at cards for many hours every day. The custom is wellnigh gone out among us now, but fifty years ago was general, fifty years before that almost universal, in the country. "Gaming has become so much the fashion," writes Seymour, the author of the Court Gamester, "that he who in company should be ignorant of the games in vogue, would be reckoned low-bred, and hardly fit for conversation." There were cards everywhere. It was considered ill-bred to read in company. "Books were not fit articles for drawing-rooms," old ladies used to say. People were jealous, as it were, and angry with them. You will find in Hervey that George II was always furious at the sight of books; and his queen, who loved reading, had to practise it in secret in her closet. But cards were the resource of all the world. Every night, for hours, kings and queens of England sat down and handled their majesties of spades and diamonds. In European Courts, I believe the practice still remains, not for gambling, but for pastime. Our ancestors generally adopted it. "Books! prithee, don't talk to me about books," said old Sarah Marlborough. "The only books I know are men and cards." "Dear old Sir Roger de Coverley sent all his tenants a string of hogs' puddings and a pack of cards at Christmas," says the Spectator, wishing to depict a kind landlord. One of the good old lady writers in whose letters I have been dipping cries out, "Sure, cards have kept us women from a great deal of scandal!" Wise old Johnson regretted that he had not learnt to play. "It is very useful in life," he says; "it generates kindness, and consolidates society." David Hume never went to bed without his whist. We have Walpole, in one of his letters, in a transport of gratitude for the cards. "I shall build an order to Pam," says he, in his pleasant dandified way, "for the escape of my charming Duchess of Grafton." The duchess had been playing cards at Rome, when she ought to have been at a cardinal's concert, where the floor fell in, and all the monsignors were precipitated into the cellar. Even the Nonconformist clergy looked not unkindly on the practice. "I do not think," says one of them, "that honest Martin Luther committed sin by playing at backgammon for an hour or two after dinner, in order by unbending his mind to promote digestion." As for the High Church parsons, they all played, bishops and all. On Twelfth Day the Court used to play in state. "This being Twelfth Day, his Majesty, the Prince of Wales, and the Knights Companions of the Garter, Thistle, and Bath, appeared in the collars of their respective orders. Their Majesties, the Prince of Wales, and three eldest Princesses, went to the Chapel Royal, preceded by the heralds. The Duke of Manchester carried the sword of state. The king and prince made offering at the altar of gold, frankincense, and myrrh, according to the annual custom. At night their Majesties played at hazard with the nobility, for the benefit of the groom-porter; and 'twas said the king won 600 guineas; the queen, 360; Princess Amelia, twenty; Princess Caroline, ten; the Duke of Grafton and the Earl of Portmore, several thousands."

Let us glance at the same chronicle, which is of the year 1731, and see how others of our forefathers were engaged.

"Cork, 15th January.—This day, one Tim Croneen was, for the murder and robbery of Mr. St. Leger and his wife, sentenced to be hanged two minutes, then his head to be cut off, and his body divided in four quarters, to be placed in four crossways. He was servant to Mr. St. Leger, and committed the murder with the privity of the servant-maid, who was sentenced to be burned; also of the gardener, whom he knocked on the head, to deprive him of his share of the booty."

"January 3.—A postboy was shot by an Irish gentleman on the road near Stone, in Staffordshire, who died in two days, for which the gentleman was imprisoned."

"A poor man was found hanging in a gentleman's stables at Bungay, in Norfolk, by a person who cut him down, and running for assistance, left his penknife behind him. The poor man recovering, cut his throat with the knife; and a river being nigh, jumped into it; but company coming, he was dragged out alive, and was like to remain so."

"The Honourable Thomas Finch, brother to the Earl of Nottingham, is appointed ambassador at the Hague, in the room of the Earl of Chesterfield, who is on his return home."

"William Cowper, Esq., and the Rev. Mr. John Cowper, chaplain in ordinary to her Majesty, and rector of Great Berkhampstead, in the county of Hertford, are appointed clerks of the commissioners of bankruptcy."

"Charles Creagh, Esq., and — Macnamara, Esq., between whom an old grudge of three years had subsisted, which had occasioned their being bound over about fifty times for breaking the peace, meeting in company with Mr. Eyres, of Galloway, they discharged their pistols, and all three were killed on the spot—to the great joy of their peaceful neighbours, say the Irish papers."

"Wheat is 26s. to 28s., and barley 20s. to 22s. a quarter; three per cents, 92; best loaf sugar, 9-1/4d.; Bohea, 12s. to 14s.; Pekoe, 18s., and Hyson, 35s. per pound."

"At Exon was celebrated with great magnificence the birthday of the son of Sir W. Courtney, Bart., at which more than 1,000 persons were present. A bullock was roasted whole; a butt of wine and several tuns of beer and cider were given to the populace. At the same time Sir William delivered to his son, then of age, Powdram Castle, and a great estate."

"Charlesworth and Cox, two solicitors, convicted of forgery, stood on the pillory at the Royal Exchange. The first was severely handled by the populace, but the other was very much favoured, and protected by six or seven fellows who got on the pillory to protect him from the insults of the mob."

"A boy killed by falling upon iron spikes, from a lamppost, which he climbed to see Mother Needham stand in the pillory."

"Mary Lynn was burned to ashes at the stake for being concerned in the murder of her mistress."

"Alexander Russell, the foot soldier, who was capitally convicted for a street robbery in January sessions, was reprieved for transportation; but having an estate fallen to him, obtained a free pardon."

"The Lord John Russell married to the Lady Diana Spencer, at Marlborough House. He has a fortune of 30,000 l. down, and is to have 100,000 l. at the death of the Duchess Dowager of Marlborough, his grandmother."

"March 1 being the anniversary of the queen's birthday, when her Majesty entered the forty-ninth year of her age, there was a splendid appearance of nobility at St. James's. Her Majesty was magnificently dressed, and wore a flowered muslin head-edging, as did also her Royal Highness. The Lord Portmore was said to have had the richest dress, though an Italian Count had twenty-four diamonds instead of buttons."

New clothes on the birthday were the fashion for all loyal people. Swift mentions the custom several times. Walpole is constantly speaking of it; laughing at the practice, but having the very finest clothes from Paris, nevertheless. If the king and queen were unpopular, there were very few new clothes at the Drawing-room. In a paper in the True Patriot, No. 3, written to attack the Pretender, the Scotch, French, and Popery, Fielding supposes the Scotch and the Pretender in possession of London, and himself about to be hanged for loyalty,—when, just as the rope is round his neck, he says: "My little girl entered my bedchamber, and put an end to my dream by pulling open my eyes, and telling me that the tailor had just brought home my clothes for his Majesty's birthday." In his Temple Beau, the beau is dunned for a birthday suit of velvet, 40 l. Be sure that Mr. Harry Fielding was dunned too.

The public days, no doubt, were splendid, but the private Court life must have been awfully wearisome. "I will not trouble you," writes Hervey to Lady Sundon, "with any account of our occupations at Hampton Court. No mill-horse ever went in a more constant track, or a more unchanging circle; so that by the assistance of an almanac for the day of the week, and a watch for the hour of the day, you may inform yourself fully, without any other intelligence but your memory, of every transaction within the verge of the Court. Walking, chaises, levées, and audiences fill the morning. At night the king plays at commerce and backgammon, and the queen at quadrille, where poor Lady Charlotte runs her usual nightly gauntlet, the queen pulling her hood, and the Princess Royal rapping her knuckles. The Duke of Grafton takes his nightly opiate of lottery, and sleeps as usual between the Princesses Amelia and Caroline. Lord Grantham strolls from one room to another (as Dryden says), like some discontented ghost that oft appears, and is forbid to speak; and stirs himself about as people stir a fire, not with any design, but in hopes to make it burn brisker. At last the king gets up; the pool finishes; and everybody has their dismission. Their Majesties retire to Lady Charlotte and my Lord Lifford; my Lord Grantham, to Lady Frances and Mr. Clark: some to supper, some to bed; and thus the evening and the morning make the day."

The king's fondness for Hanover occasioned all sorts of rough jokes among his English subjects, to whom Sauerkraut and sausages have ever been ridiculous objects. When our present Prince Consort came among us, the people bawled out songs in the streets indicative of the absurdity of Germany in general. The sausage-shops produced enormous sausages which we might suppose were the daily food and delight of German princes. I remember the caricatures at the marriage of Prince Leopold with the Princess Charlotte. The bridegroom was drawn in rags. George III's wife was called by the people a beggarly German duchess; the British idea being that all princes were beggarly except British princes.

King George paid us back. He thought there were no manners out of Germany. Sarah Marlborough once coming to visit the princess, whilst her Royal Highness was whipping one of the roaring royal children, "Ah!" says George, who was standing by, "you have no good manners in England, because you are not properly brought up when you are young." He insisted that no English cooks could roast, no English coachman could drive: he actually questioned the superiority of our nobility, our horses, and our roast beef!

Whilst he was away from his beloved Hanover, everything remained there exactly as in the prince's presence. There were 800 horses in the stables, there was all the apparatus of chamberlains, Court-marshals, and equerries; and Court assemblies were held every Saturday, where all the nobility of Hanover assembled at what I can't but think a fine and touching ceremony. A large armchair was placed in the assembly-room, and on it the king's portrait. The nobility advanced, and made a bow to the armchair, and to the image which Nebuchadnezzar the king had set up; and spoke under their voices before the august picture, just as they would have done had the King Churfürst been present himself.

He was always going back to Hanover. In the year 1729, he went for two whole years, during which Caroline reigned for him in England, and he was not in the least missed by his British subjects. He went again in '35 and '36; and between the years 1740 and 1755 was no less than eight times on the Continent, which amusement he was obliged to give up at the outbreak of the Seven Years' War. Here every day's amusement was the same. "Our life is as uniform as that of a monastery," writes a courtier whom Vehse quotes. "Every morning at eleven, and every evening at six, we drive in the heat to Herrenhausen, through an enormous linden avenue; and twice a day cover our coats and coaches with dust. In the king's society there never is the least change. At table, and at cards, he sees always the same faces, and at the end of the game retires into his chamber. Twice a week there is a French theatre; the other days there is play in the gallery. In this way, were the king always to stop in Hanover, one could make a ten years' calendar of his proceedings; and settle beforehand what his time of business, meals, and pleasure would be."

The old pagan kept his promise to his dying wife. Lady Yarmouth was now in full favour, and treated with profound respect by the Hanover society, though it appears rather neglected in England when she came among us. In 1740, a couple of the king's daughters went to see him at Hanover; Anna, the Princess of Orange (about whom, and whose husband and marriage-day, Walpole and Hervey have left us the most ludicrous descriptions), and Maria of Hesse-Cassel, with their respective lords. This made the Hanover Court very brilliant. In honour of his high guests, the king gave several fêtes; among others, a magnificent masked ball, in the green theatre at Herrenhausen—the garden theatre, with linden and box for screen, and grass for a carpet, where the Platens had danced to George and his father the late sultan. The stage and a great part of the garden were illuminated with coloured lamps. Almost the whole Court appeared in white dominos, "like," says the describer of the scene, "like spirits in the Elysian fields. At night, supper was served in the gallery with three great tables, and the king was very merry. After supper dancing was resumed, and I did not get home till five o'clock by full daylight to Hanover. Some days afterwards we had in the opera-house at Hanover, a great assembly. The king appeared in a Turkish dress; his turban was ornamented with a magnificent agraffe of diamonds; the Lady Yarmouth was dressed as a sultana; nobody was more beautiful than the Princess of Hesse." So, while poor Caroline was resting in her coffin, dapper little George, with his red face and his white eyebrows and goggle-eyes, at sixty years of age, is dancing a pretty dance with Madame Walmoden, and capering about dressed up like a Turk! For twenty years more, that little old Bajazet went on in this Turkish fashion, until the fit came which choked the old man, when he ordered the side of his coffin to be taken out, as well as that of poor Caroline's who had preceded him, so that his sinful old bones and ashes might mingle with those of the faithful creature. O strutting Turkey-cock of Herrenhausen! O naughty little Mahomet! in what Turkish paradise are you now, and where be your painted houris? So Countess Yarmouth appeared as a sultana, and his Majesty in a Turkish dress wore an agraffe of diamonds, and was very merry, was he? Friends! he was your fathers' king as well as mine—let us drop a respectful tear over his grave.

He said of his wife that he never knew a woman who was worthy to buckle her shoe: he would sit alone weeping before her portrait, and when he had dried his eyes, he would go off to his Walmoden and talk of her. On the 25th day of October, 1760, he being then in the seventy-seventh year of his age, and the thirty-fourth of his reign, his page went to take him his royal chocolate, and behold! the most religious and gracious king was lying dead on the floor. They went and fetched Walmoden; but Walmoden could not wake him. The sacred Majesty was but a lifeless corpse. The king was dead; God save the king! But, of course, poets and clergymen decorously bewailed the late one. Here are some artless verses, in which an English divine deplored the famous departed hero, and over which you may cry or you may laugh, exactly as your humour suits:—

While at his feet expiring Faction lay,
No contest left but who should best obey;
Saw in his offspring all himself renewed;
The same fair path of glory still pursued;
Saw to young George Augusta's care impart
Whate'er could raise and humanize the heart;
Blend all his grandsire's virtues with his own,
And form their mingled radiance for the throne—
No farther blessing could on earth be given—
The next degree of happiness was—heaven!

If he had been good, if he had been just, if he had been pure in life, and wise in council, could the poet have said much more? It was a parson who came and wept over this grave, with Walmoden sitting on it, and claimed heaven for the poor old man slumbering below. Here was one who had neither dignity, learning, morals, nor wit—who tainted a great society by a bad example; who in youth, manhood, old age, was gross, low, and sensual; and Mr. Porteus, afterwards my Lord Bishop Porteus, says the earth was not good enough for him, and that his only place was heaven! Bravo, Mr. Porteus! The divine who wept these tears over George II's memory wore George III's lawn. I don't know whether people still admire his poetry or his sermons.

George The Third

We have to glance over sixty years in as many minutes. To read the mere catalogue of characters who figured during that long period, would occupy our allotted time, and we should have all text and no sermon. England has to undergo the revolt of the American colonies; to submit to defeat and separation; to shake under the volcano of the French Revolution; to grapple and fight for the life with her gigantic enemy Napoleon; to gasp and rally after that tremendous struggle. The old society, with its courtly splendours, has to pass away; generations of statesmen to rise and disappear; Pitt to follow Chatham to the tomb; the memory of Rodney and Wolfe to be superseded by Nelson's and Wellington's glory; the old poets who unite us to Queen Anne's time to sink into their graves; Johnson to die, and

Scott and Byron to arise; Garrick to delight the world with his dazzling dramatic genius, and Kean to leap on the stage and take possession of the astonished theatre. Steam has to be invented; kings to be beheaded, banished, deposed, restored. Napoleon to be but an episode, and George III is to be alive through all these varied changes, to accompany his people through all these revolutions of thought, government, society; to survive out of the old world into ours.

When I first saw England, she was in mourning for the young Princess Charlotte, the hope of the empire. I came from India as a child, and our ship touched at an island on the way home, where my black servant took me a long walk over rocks and hills until we reached a garden, where we saw a man walking. "That is he," said the black man: "that is Bonaparte! He eats three sheep every day, and all the little children he can lay hands on!" There were people in the British dominions besides that poor Calcutta serving-man, with an equal horror of the Corsican ogre.

With the same childish attendant, I remember peeping through the colonnade at Carlton House, and seeing the abode of the great Prince Regent. I can see yet the Guards pacing before the gates of the place. The place? What place? The palace exists no more than the palace of Nebuchadnezzar. It is but a name now. Where be the sentries who used to salute as the Royal chariots drove in and out? The chariots, with the kings inside, have driven to the realms of Pluto; the tall Guards have marched into darkness, and the echoes of their drums are rolling in Hades. Where the palace once stood, a hundred little children are paddling up and down the steps to St. James's Park. A score of grave gentlemen are taking their tea at the Athenaeum Club; as many grizzly warriors are garrisoning the United Service Club opposite. Pall Mall is the great social Exchange of London now—the mart of news, of politics, of scandal, of rumour—the English forum, so to speak, where men discuss the last dispatch from the Crimea, the last speech of Lord Derby, the next move of Lord John. And, now and then, to a few antiquarians, whose thoughts are with the past rather than with the present, it is a memorial of old times and old people, and Pall Mall is our Palmyra. Look! About this spot, Tom of Ten Thousand was killed by Königsmarck's gang. In that great red house Gainsborough lived, and Culloden Cumberland, George III's uncle. Yonder is Sarah Marlborough's palace, just as it stood when that termagant occupied it. At 25, Walter Scott used to live; at the house, now No. 79, and occupied by the Society for the Propagation of the Gospel in Foreign Parts, resided Mrs. Eleanor Gwynn, comedian.

How often has Queen Caroline's chair issued from under yonder arch! All the men of the Georges have passed up and down the street. It has seen Walpole's chariot and Chatham's sedan; and Fox, Gibbon, Sheridan, on their way to Brookes's; and stately William Pitt stalking on the arm of Dundas; and Hanger and Tom Sheridan reeling out of Raggett's; and Byron limping into Wattier's; and Swift striding out of Bury Street; and Mr. Addison and Dick Steele, both perhaps a little the better for liquor; and the Prince of Wales and the Duke of York clattering over the pavement; and Johnson counting the posts along the streets, after dawdling before Dodsley's window; and Horry Walpole hobbling into his carriage, with a gimcrack just bought out at Christie's; and George Selwyn sauntering into White's.

In the published letters to George Selwyn we get a mass of correspondence by no means so brilliant and witty as Walpole's, or so bitter and bright as Hervey's, but as interesting, and even more descriptive of the time, because the letters are the work of many hands. You hear more voices speaking, as it were, and more natural than Horace's dandified treble, and Sporus's malignant whisper. As one reads the Selwyn letters—as one looks at Reynolds's noble pictures illustrative of those magnificent times and voluptuous people—one almost hears the voice of the dead past; the laughter and the chorus; the toast called over the brimming cups; the shout at the racecourse or the gaming-table; the merry joke frankly spoken to the laughing fine lady. How fine those ladies were, those ladies who heard and spoke such coarse jokes; how grand those gentlemen!

I fancy that peculiar product of the past, the fine gentleman, has almost vanished off the face of the earth, and is disappearing like the beaver or the Red Indian. We can't have fine gentlemen any more, because we can't have the society in which they lived. The people will not obey: the parasites will not be as obsequious as formerly: children do not go down on their knees to beg their parents' blessing: chaplains do not say grace and retire before the pudding: servants do not say "your honour" and "your worship" at every moment: tradesmen do not stand hat in hand as the gentleman passes: authors do not wait for hours in gentlemen's ante-rooms with a fulsome dedication, for which they hope to get five guineas from his lordship. In the days when there were fine gentlemen, Mr. Secretary Pitt's under-secretaries did not dare to sit down before him; but Mr. Pitt, in his turn, went down on his gouty knees to George II; and when George III spoke a few kind words to him, Lord Chatham burst into tears of reverential joy and gratitude; so awful was the idea of the monarch, and so great the distinctions of rank. Fancy Lord John Russell or Lord Palmerston on their knees whilst the sovereign was reading a dispatch, or beginning to cry because Prince Albert said something civil!

At the accession of George III, the patricians were yet at the height of their good fortune. Society recognized their superiority, which they themselves pretty calmly took for granted. They inherited not only titles and estates, and seats in the House of Peers, but seats in the House of Commons. There were a multitude of Government places, and not merely these, but bribes of actual 500 l. notes, which Members of the House took not much shame in assuming. Fox went into Parliament at 20: Pitt was just of age: his father not much older. It was the good time for Patricians. Small blame to them if they took and enjoyed, and over-enjoyed, the prizes of politics, the pleasures of social life.

In these letters to Selwyn, we are made acquainted with a whole society of these defunct fine gentlemen: and can watch with a curious interest a life, which the novel-writers of that time, I think, have scarce touched upon. To Smollett, to Fielding even, a lord was a lord: a gorgeous being with a blue ribbon, a coroneted chair, and an immense star on his bosom, to whom commoners paid reverence. Richardson, a man of humbler birth than either of the above two, owned that he was ignorant regarding the manners of the aristocracy, and besought Mrs. Donnellan, a lady who had lived in the great world, to examine a volume of Sir Charles Grandison, and point out any errors which she might see in this particular. Mrs. Donnellan found so many faults, that Richardson changed colour; shut up the book; and muttered that it were best to throw it in the fire. Here, in Selwyn, we have the real original men and women of fashion of the early time of George III. We can follow them to the new club at Almack's: we can travel over Europe with them: we can accompany them not only to the public places, but to their country-houses and private society. Here is a whole company of them; wits and prodigals; some persevering in their bad ways; some repentant, but relapsing; beautiful ladies, parasites, humble chaplains, led captains. Those fair creatures whom we love in Reynolds's portraits, and who still look out on us from his canvases with their sweet calm faces and gracious smiles—those fine gentlemen who did us the honour to govern us; who inherited their boroughs; took their ease in their patent places; and slipped Lord North's bribes so elegantly under their ruffles—we make acquaintance with a hundred of these fine folks, hear their talk and laughter, read of their loves, quarrels, intrigues, debts, duels, divorces; can fancy them alive if we read the book long enough. We can attend at Duke Hamilton's wedding, and behold him marry his bride with the curtain-ring: we can peep into her poor sister's death-bed: we can see Charles Fox cursing over the cards, or March bawling out the odds at Newmarket: we can imagine Burgoyne tripping off from St. James's Street to conquer the Americans, and slinking back into the club somewhat crestfallen after his beating: we can see the young king dressing himself for the

Drawing-room and asking ten thousand questions regarding all the gentlemen: we can have high life or low, the struggle at the Opera to behold the Violetta or the Zamperini—the Macaronis and fine ladies in their chairs trooping to the masquerade or Madame Cornelys's—the crowd at Drury Lane to look at the body of Miss Ray, whom Parson Hackman has just pistolled—or we can peep into Newgate, where poor Mr. Rice the forger is waiting his fate and his supper. "You need not be particular about the sauce for his fowl," says one turnkey to another: "for you know he is to be hanged in the morning." "Yes," replies the second janitor, "but the chaplain sups with him, and he is a terrible fellow for melted butter."

Selwyn has a chaplain and parasite, one Dr. Warner, than whom Plautus, or Ben Jonson, or Hogarth, never painted a better character. In letter after letter he adds fresh strokes to the portrait of himself, and completes a portrait not a little curious to look at now that the man has passed away; all the foul pleasures and gambols in which he revelled, played out; all the rouged faces into which he leered, worms and skulls; all the fine gentlemen whose shoebuckles he kissed, laid in their coffins. This worthy clergyman takes care to tell us that he does not believe in his religion, though, thank Heaven, he is not so great a rogue as a lawyer. He goes on Mr. Selwyn's errands, any errands, and is proud, he says, to be that gentleman's proveditor. He waits upon the Duke of Queensberry—old Q.—and exchanges pretty stories with that aristocrat. He comes home "after a hard day's christening", as he says, and writes to his patron before sitting down to whist and partridges for supper. He revels in the thoughts of ox-cheek and burgundy—he is a boisterous, uproarious parasite, licks his master's shoes with explosions of laughter and cunning smack and gusto, and likes the taste of that blacking as much as the best claret in old Q.'s cellar. He has Rabelais and Horace at his greasy fingers' ends. He is inexpressibly mean, curiously jolly; kindly and good-natured in secret—a tender-hearted knave, not a venomous lickspittle. Jesse says, that at his chapel in Long Acre, "he attained a considerable popularity by the pleasing, manly, and eloquent style of his delivery." Was infidelity endemic, and corruption in the air? Around a young king, himself of the most exemplary life and undoubted piety, lived a Court society as dissolute as our country ever knew. George II's bad morals bore their fruit in George III's early years; as I believe that a knowledge of that good man's example, his moderation, his frugal simplicity, and God-fearing life, tended infinitely to improve the morals of the country and purify the whole nation.

After Warner, the most interesting of Selwyn's correspondents is the Earl of Carlisle, grandfather of the amiable nobleman at present Viceroy in Ireland. The grandfather, too, was Irish Viceroy, having previously been treasurer of the king's household; and, in 1778, the principal commissioner for treating, consulting, and agreeing upon the means of quieting the divisions subsisting in his Majesty's colonies, plantations, and possessions in North America. You may read his lordship's manifestos in the Royal New York Gazette. He returned to England, having by no means quieted the colonies; and speedily afterwards the Royal New York Gazette somehow ceased to be published.

This good, clever, kind, highly-bred Lord Carlisle was one of the English fine gentlemen who were wellnigh ruined by the awful debauchery and extravagance which prevailed in the great English society of those days. Its dissoluteness was awful: it had swarmed over Europe after the Peace; it had danced, and raced, and gambled in all the Courts. It had made its bow at Versailles; it had run its horses on the plain of Sablons, near Paris, and created the Anglomania there: it had exported vast quantities of pictures and marbles from Rome and Florence: it had ruined itself by building great galleries and palaces for the reception of the statues and pictures: it had brought over singing-women and dancing-women from all the operas of Europe, on whom my lords lavished their thousands, whilst they left their honest wives and honest children languishing in the lonely, deserted splendours of the castle and park at home.

Besides the great London society of those days, there was another unacknowledged world, extravagant beyond measure, tearing about in the pursuit of pleasure; dancing, gambling, drinking, singing; meeting the real society in the public places (at Ranelaghs, Vauxhalls, and Ridottos, about which our old novelists talk so constantly), and outvying the real leaders of fashion, in luxury, and splendour, and beauty. For instance, when the famous Miss Gunning visited Paris as Lady Coventry, where she expected that her beauty would meet with the applause which had followed her and her sister through England, it appears she was put to flight by an English lady still more lovely in the eyes of the Parisians. A certain Mrs. Pitt took a box at the opera opposite the countess; and was so much handsomer than her ladyship, that the parterre cried out that this was the real English angel, whereupon Lady Coventry quitted Paris in a huff. The poor thing died presently of consumption, accelerated, it was said, by the red and white paint with which she plastered those luckless charms of hers. (We must represent to ourselves all fashionable female Europe, at that time, as plastered with white, and raddled with red.) She left two daughters behind her, whom George Selwyn loved (he was curiously fond of little children), and who are described very drolly and pathetically in these letters, in their little nursery, where passionate little Lady Fanny, if she had not good cards, flung hers into Lady Mary's face; and where they sat conspiring how they should receive a new mother-in-law whom their papa presently brought home. They got on very well with their mother-in-law, who was very kind to them; and they grew up, and they were married, and they were both divorced afterwards—poor little souls! Poor painted mother, poor society, ghastly in its pleasures, its loves, its revelries!

As for my lord commissioner, we can afford to speak about him: because, though he was a wild and weak commissioner at one time, though he hurt his estate, though he gambled and lost ten thousand pounds at a sitting—"five times more," says the unlucky gentleman, "than I ever lost before;" though he swore he never would touch a card again; and yet, strange to say, went back to the table and lost still more: yet he repented of his errors, sobered down, and became a worthy peer and a good country gentleman, and returned to the good wife and the good children whom he had always loved with the best part of his heart. He had married at one-and-twenty. He found himself, in the midst of a dissolute society, at the head of a great fortune. Forced into luxury, and obliged to be a great lord and a great idler, he yielded to some temptations, and paid for them a bitter penalty of manly remorse; from some others he fled wisely, and ended by conquering them nobly. But he always had the good wife and children in his mind, and they saved him. "I am very glad you did not come to me the morning I left London," he writes to G. Selwyn, as he is embarking for America. "I can only say, I never knew till that moment of parting, what grief was." There is no parting now, where they are. The faithful wife, the kind, generous gentleman, have left a noble race behind them: an inheritor of his name and titles, who is beloved as widely as he is known; a man most kind, accomplished, gentle, friendly, and pure; and female descendants occupying high stations and embellishing great names; some renowned for beauty, and all for spotless lives, and pious matronly virtues.

Another of Selwyn's correspondents is the Earl of March, afterwards Duke of Queensberry, whose life lasted into this century; and who certainly as earl or duke, young man or greybeard, was not an ornament to any possible society. The legends about old Q. are awful. In Selwyn, in Wraxall, and contemporary chronicles, the observer of human nature may follow him, drinking, gambling, intriguing to the end of his career; when the wrinkled, palsied, toothless old Don Juan died, as wicked and unrepentant as he had been at the hottest season of youth and passion. There is a house in Piccadilly, where they used to show a certain low window at which old Q. sat to his very last days, ogling through his senile glasses the women as they passed by.

There must have been a great deal of good about this lazy, sleepy George Selwyn, which, no doubt, is set to his present credit. "Your friendship," writes Carlisle to him, "is so different from anything I have ever met with or seen in the world, that when I recollect the extraordinary proofs of your kindness, it seems to me like a dream." "I have lost my oldest friend, and acquaintance, G. Selwyn," writes Walpole to Miss Berry: "I really loved him, not only for his infinite wit, but for a thousand good qualities." I am glad, for my part, that such a lover of cakes and ale should have had a thousand good qualities—that he should have been friendly, generous, warm-hearted, trustworthy. "I rise at six," writes Carlisle to him, from Spa (a great resort of fashionable people in our ancestors' days), "play at cricket till dinner, and dance in the evening, till I can scarcely crawl to bed at eleven. There is a life for you! You get up at nine; play with Raton your dog till twelve, in your dressing-gown; then creep down to White's; are five hours at table; sleep till supper-time; and then make two wretches carry you in a sedan-chair, with three pints of claret in you, three miles for a shilling." Occasionally, instead of sleeping at White's, George went down and snoozed in the House of Commons by the side of Lord North. He represented Gloucester for many years, and had a borough of his own, Ludgershall, for which, when he was too lazy to contest Gloucester, he sat himself. "I have given directions for the election of Ludgershall to be of Lord Melbourne and myself," he writes to the Premier, whose friend he was, and who was himself as sleepy, as witty, and as good-natured as George.

If, in looking at the lives of princes, courtiers, men of rank and fashion, we must perforce depict them as idle, profligate, and criminal, we must make allowances for the rich men's failings, and recollect that we, too, were very likely indolent and voluptuous, had we no motive for work, a mortal's natural taste for pleasure, and the daily temptation of a large income. What could a great peer, with a great castle and park, and a great fortune, do but be splendid and idle? In these letters of Lord Carlisle's from which I have been quoting, there is many a just complaint made by the kind-hearted young nobleman of the state which he is obliged to keep; the magnificence in which he must live; the idleness to which his position as a peer of England bound him. Better for him had he been a lawyer at his desk, or a clerk in his office;—a thousand times better chance for happiness, education, employment, security from temptation. A few years since the profession of arms was the only one which our nobles could follow. The Church, the Bar, medicine, literature, the arts, commerce, were below them. It is to the middle class we must look for the safety of England: the working educated men, away from Lord North's bribery in the senate; the good clergy not corrupted into parasites by hopes of preferment; the tradesmen rising into manly opulence; the painters pursuing their gentle calling; the men of letters in their quiet studies; these are the men whom we love and like to read of in the last age. How small the grandees and the men of pleasure look beside them! how contemptible the story of the George III Court squabbles are beside the recorded talk of dear old Johnson! What is the grandest entertainment at Windsor, compared to a night at the club over its modest cups, with Percy and Langton, and Goldsmith, and poor Bozzy at the table? I declare I think, of all the polite men of that age, Joshua Reynolds was the finest gentleman. And they were good, as well as witty and wise, those dear old friends of the past. Their minds were not debauched by excess, or effeminate with luxury. They toiled their noble day's labour: they rested, and took their kindly pleasure: they cheered their holiday meetings with generous wit and hearty interchange of thought: they were no prudes, but no blush need follow their conversation: they were merry, but no riot came out of their cups. Ah! I would have liked a night at the "Turk's Head", even though bad news had arrived from the colonies, and Doctor Johnson was growling against the rebels; to have sat with him and Goldy; and to have heard Burke, the finest talker in the world; and to have had Garrick flashing in with a story from his theatre!—I like, I say, to think of that society; and not merely how pleasant and how wise, but how good they were. I think it was on going home one night from the club that Edmund Burke—his noble soul full of great thoughts, be sure, for they never left him; his heart full of gentleness—was accosted by a poor wandering woman, to whom he spoke words of kindness;

and moved by the tears of this Magdalen, perhaps having caused them by the good words he spoke to her, he took her home to the house of his wife and children, and never left her until he had found the means of restoring her to honesty and labour. O you fine gentlemen! you Marches, and Selwyns, and Chesterfields, how small you look by the side of these great men! Good-natured Carlisle plays at cricket all day, and dances in the evening "till he can scarcely crawl", gaily contrasting his superior virtue with George Selwyn's "carried to bed by two wretches at midnight with three pints of claret in him". Do you remember the verses—the sacred verses—which Johnson wrote on the death of his humble friend, Levett?

Well tried through many a varying year,
See Levett to the grave descend;
Officious, innocent, sincere,
Of every friendless name the friend.

In misery's darkest cavern known,
His useful care was ever nigh,
Where hopeless anguish poured the groan,
And lonely want retired to die.

No summons mocked by chill delay,
No petty gain disdained by pride,
The modest wants of every day
The toil of every day supplied.

His virtues walked their narrow round,
Nor made a pause, nor left a void:
And sure the Eternal Master found
His single talent well employed.

Whose name looks the brightest now, that of Queensberry the wealthy duke, or Selwyn the wit, or Levett the poor physician?

I hold old Johnson (and shall we not pardon James Boswell some errors for embalming him for us?) to be the great supporter of the British Monarchy and Church during the last age—better than whole benches of bishops, better than Pitts, Norths, and the great Burke himself. Johnson had the ear of the nation: his immense authority reconciled it to loyalty, and shamed it out of irreligion. When George III talked with him, and the people heard the great author's good opinion of the sovereign, whole generations rallied to the king. Johnson was revered as a sort of oracle; and the oracle declared for Church and King. What a humanity the old man had! He was a kindly partaker of all honest pleasures: a fierce foe to all sin, but a gentle enemy to all sinners. "What, boys, are you for a frolic?" he cries, when Topham Beauclerc comes and wakes him up at midnight: "I'm with you," And away he goes, tumbles on his homely old clothes, and trundles through Covent Garden with the young fellows. When he used to frequent Garrick's theatre, and had "the liberty of the scenes", he says, "all the actresses knew me, and dropped me a curtsy as they passed to the stage." That would make a pretty picture: it is a pretty picture in my mind, of youth, folly, gaiety, tenderly surveyed by wisdom's merciful, pure eyes.

George III and his queen lived in a very unpretending but elegant-looking house, on the site of the hideous pile under which his granddaughter at present reposes. The king's mother inhabited Carlton

House, which contemporary prints represent with a perfect paradise of a garden, with trim lawns, green arcades, and vistas of classic statues. She admired these in company with my Lord Bute, who had a fine classic taste, and sometimes counsel took and sometimes tea in the pleasant green arbours along with that polite nobleman. Bute was hated with a rage of which there have been few examples in English history. He was the butt for everybody's abuse; for Wilkes's devilish mischief; for Churchill's slashing satire; for the hooting of the mob that roasted the boot, his emblem, in a thousand bonfires; that hated him because he was a favourite and a Scotchman, calling him "Mortimer", "Lothario", I know not what names, and accusing his royal mistress of all sorts of crimes—the grave, lean, demure, elderly woman, who, I dare say, was quite as good as her neighbours. Chatham lent the aid of his great malice to influence the popular sentiment against her. He assailed, in the House of Lords, "the secret influence, more mighty than the Throne itself, which betrayed and clogged every administration." The most furious pamphlets echoed the cry. "Impeach the king's mother," was scribbled over every wall at the Court end of the town, Walpole tells us. What had she done? What had Frederick, Prince of Wales, George's father, done, that he was so loathed by George II and never mentioned by George III? Let us not seek for stones to batter that forgotten grave, but acquiesce in the contemporary epitaph over him:—

Here lies Fred,
Who was alive, and is dead.
Had it been his father,
I had much rather.
Had it been his brother,
Still better than another.
Had it been his sister,
No one would have missed her.
Had it been the whole generation,
Still better for the nation.
But since 'tis only Fred,
Who was alive, and is dead,
There's no more to be said.

The widow with eight children round her, prudently reconciled herself with the king, and won the old man's confidence and goodwill. A shrewd, hard, domineering, narrow-minded woman, she educated her children according to her lights, and spoke of the eldest as a dull, good boy: she kept him very close: she held the tightest rein over him: she had curious prejudices and bigotries. His uncle, the burly Cumberland, taking down a sabre once, and drawing it to amuse the child—the boy started back and turned pale. The prince felt a generous shock: "What must they have told him about me?" he asked.

His mother's bigotry and hatred he inherited with the courageous obstinacy of his own race; but he was a firm believer where his fathers had been freethinkers, and a true and fond supporter of the Church, of which he was the titular defender. Like other dull men, the king was all his life suspicious of superior people. He did not like Fox; he did not like Reynolds; he did not like Nelson, Chatham, Burke; he was testy at the idea of all innovations, and suspicious of all innovators. He loved mediocrities; Benjamin West was his favourite painter; Beattie was his poet. The king lamented, not without pathos, in his after-life, that his education had been neglected. He was a dull lad brought up by narrow-minded people. The cleverest tutors in the world could have done little probably to expand that small intellect, though they might have improved his tastes, and taught his perceptions some generosity.

But he admired as well as he could. There is little doubt that a letter, written by the little Princess Charlotte of Mecklenburg-Strelitz,—a letter containing the most feeble commonplaces about the horrors of war, and the most trivial remarks on the blessings of peace, struck the young monarch greatly, and decided him upon selecting the young princess as the sharer of his throne, I pass over the stories of his juvenile loves—of Hannah Lightfoot, the Quaker, to whom they say he was actually married (though I don't know who has ever seen the register)—of lovely black-haired Sarah Lennox, about whose beauty Walpole has written in raptures, and who used to lie in wait for the young prince, and make hay at him on the lawn of Holland House. He sighed and he longed, but he rode away from her. Her picture still hangs in Holland House, a magnificent masterpiece of Reynolds, a canvas worthy of Titian. She looks from the castle window, holding a bird in her hand, at black-eyed young Charles Fox, her nephew. The royal bird flew away from lovely Sarah. She had to figure as bridesmaid at her little Mecklenburg rival's wedding, and died in our own time a quiet old lady, who had become the mother of the heroic Napiers.

They say the little princess who had written the fine letter about the horrors of war—a beautiful letter without a single blot, for which she was to be rewarded, like the heroine of the old spelling-book story—was at play one day with some of her young companions in the gardens of Strelitz, and that the young ladies' conversation was, strange to say, about husbands. "Who will take such a poor little princess as me?" Charlotte said to her friend, Ida von Bulow, and at that very moment the postman's horn sounded, and Ida said, "Princess! there is the sweetheart." As she said, so it actually turned out. The postman brought letters from the splendid young King of all England, who said, "Princess! because you have written such a beautiful letter, which does credit to your head and heart, come and be Queen of Great Britain, France, and Ireland, and the true wife of your most obedient servant, George!" So she jumped for joy; and went upstairs and packed all her little trunks; and set off straightway for her kingdom in a beautiful yacht, with a harpsichord on board for her to play upon, and around her a beautiful fleet, all covered with flags and streamers, and the distinguished Madame Auerbach complimented her with an ode, a translation of which may be read in the Gentleman's Magazine to the present day:—

Her gallant navy through the main,
Now cleaves its liquid way.
There to their queen a chosen train
Of nymphs due reverence pay.

Europa, when conveyed by Jove
To Crete's distinguished shore,
Greater attention scarce could prove,
Or be respected more.

They met, and they were married, and for years they led the happiest, simplest lives sure ever led by married couple. It is said the king winced when he first saw his homely little bride; but, however that may be, he was a true and faithful husband to her, as she was a faithful and loving wife. They had the simplest pleasures—the very mildest and simplest—little country dances, to which a dozen couple were invited, and where the honest king would stand up and dance for three hours at a time to one tune; after which delicious excitement they would go to bed without any supper (the Court people grumbling sadly at that absence of supper), and get up quite early the next morning, and perhaps the next night have another dance; or the queen would play on the spinet—she played pretty well, Haydn said—or the king would read to her a paper out of the Spectator, or perhaps one of Ogden's sermons. O Arcadia! what a life it must have been! There used to be Sunday drawing-rooms at Court; but the young king stopped these, as he stopped all that godless gambling whereof we have made mention. Not that George was averse to any innocent pleasures, or pleasures which he thought innocent. He was a patron of the arts, after his fashion; kind and gracious to the artists whom he favoured, and respectful to their calling. He wanted once to establish an Order of Minerva for literary and scientific characters; the knights were to take rank after the knights of the Bath, and to sport a straw-coloured ribbon and a star of sixteen points. But there was such a row amongst the literati as to the persons who should be appointed, that the plan was given up, and Minerva and her star never came down amongst us.

He objected to painting St. Paul's, as Popish practice; accordingly, the most clumsy heathen sculptures decorate that edifice at present. It is fortunate that the paintings, too, were spared, for painting and drawing were wofully unsound at the close of the last century; and it is far better for our eyes to contemplate whitewash (when we turn them away from the clergyman) than to look at Opie's pitchy canvases, or Fuseli's livid monsters.

And yet there is one day in the year—a day when old George loved with all his heart to attend it—when I think St. Paul's presents the noblest sight in the whole world: when five thousand charity children, with cheeks like nosegays, and sweet, fresh voices, sing the hymn which makes every heart thrill with praise and happiness. I have seen a hundred grand sights in the world—coronations, Parisian splendours, Crystal Palace openings, Pope's chapels with their processions of long-tailed cardinals and quavering choirs of fat soprani—but think in all Christendom there is no such sight as Charity Children's Day. Non Angli, sed angeli. As one looks at that beautiful multitude of innocents: as the first note strikes: indeed one may almost fancy that cherubs are singing.

Of church music the king was always very fond, showing skill in it both as a critic and a performer. Many stories, mirthful and affecting, are told of his behaviour at the concerts which he ordered. When he was blind and ill he chose the music for the Ancient Concerts once, and the music and words which he selected were from Samson Agonistes, and all had reference to his blindness, his captivity, and his affliction. He would beat time with his music-roll as they sang the anthem in the Chapel Royal. If the page below was talkative or inattentive, down would come the music-roll on young scapegrace's powdered head. The theatre was always his delight. His bishops and clergy used to attend it, thinking it no shame to appear where that good man was seen. He is said not to have cared for Shakespeare or tragedy much; farces and pantomimes were his joy; and especially when clown swallowed a carrot or a string of sausages, he would laugh so outrageously that the lovely princess by his side would have to say, "My gracious monarch, do compose yourself." But he continued to laugh, and at the very smallest farces, as long as his poor wits were left him.

There is something to me exceedingly touching in that simple early life of the king's. As long as his mother lived—a dozen years after his marriage with the little spinet-player—he was a great, shy, awkward boy, under the tutelage of that hard parent. She must have been a clever, domineering, cruel woman. She kept her household lonely and in gloom, mistrusting almost all people who came about her children. Seeing the young Duke of Gloucester silent and unhappy once, she sharply asked him the cause of his silence. "I am thinking," said the poor child. "Thinking, sir! and of what?" "I am thinking if ever I have a son I will not make him so unhappy as you make me." The other sons were all wild, except George. Dutifully every evening George and Charlotte paid their visit to the king's mother at Carlton House. She had a throat complaint, of which she died; but to the last persisted in driving about the streets to show she was alive. The night before her death the resolute woman talked with her son and daughter-in-law as usual, went to bed, and was found dead there in the morning. "George, be a king!"

were the words which she was for ever croaking in the ears of her son: and a king the simple, stubborn, affectionate, bigoted man tried to be.

He did his best; he worked according to his lights; what virtue he knew, he tried to practise; what knowledge he could master, he strove to acquire. He was for ever drawing maps, for example, and learned geography with no small care and industry. He knew all about the family histories and genealogies of his gentry, and pretty histories he must have known. He knew the whole Army List; and all the facings, and the exact number of the buttons, and all the tags and laces, and the cut of all the cocked hats, pigtails, and gaiters in his army. He knew the personnel of the Universities; what doctors were inclined to Socinianism, and who were sound Churchmen; he knew the etiquettes of his own and his grandfather's Courts to a nicety, and the smallest particulars regarding the routine of ministers, secretaries, embassies, audiences; the humblest page in the ante-room, or the meanest helper in the stables or kitchen. These parts of the royal business he was capable of learning, and he learned. But, as one thinks of an office, almost divine, performed by any mortal man—any single being pretending to control the thoughts, to direct the faith, to order the implicit obedience of brother millions, to compel them into war at his offence or quarrel; to command, "In this way you shall trade, in this way you shall think; these neighbours shall be your allies whom you shall help, these others your enemies whom you shall slay at my orders; in this way you shall worship God;"—who can wonder that, when such a man as George took such an office on himself, punishment and humiliation should fall upon people and chief?

Yet there is something grand about his courage. The battle of the king with his aristocracy remains yet to be told by the historian who shall view the reign of George more justly than the trumpery panegyrists who wrote immediately after his decease. It was he, with the people to back him, who made the war with America; it was he and the people who refused justice to the Roman Catholics; and on both questions he beat the patricians. He bribed: he bullied: he darkly dissembled on occasion: he exercised a slippery perseverance, and a vindictive resolution, which one almost admires as one thinks his character over. His courage was never to be beat. It trampled North under foot: it bent the stiff neck of the younger Pitt: even his illness never conquered that indomitable spirit. As soon as his brain was clear, it resumed the scheme, only laid aside when his reason left him: as soon as his hands were out of the strait-waistcoat, they took up the pen and the plan which had engaged him up to the moment of his malady. I believe it is by persons believing themselves in the right that nine-tenths of the tyranny of this world has been perpetrated. Arguing on that convenient premiss, the Dey of Algiers would cut off twenty heads of a morning; Father Dominic would burn a score of Jews in the presence of the most Catholic King, and the Archbishops of Toledo and Salamanca sing Amen. Protestants were roasted, Jesuits hung and quartered at Smithfield, and witches burned at Salem, and all by worthy people, who believed they had the best authority for their actions.

And so, with respect to old George, even Americans, whom he hated and who conquered him, may give him credit for having quite honest reasons for oppressing them. Appended to Lord Brougham's biographical sketch of Lord North are some autograph notes of the king, which let us most curiously into the state of his mind. "The times certainly require," says he, "the concurrence of all who wish to prevent anarchy. I have no wish but the prosperity of my own dominions, therefore I must look upon all who would not heartily assist me as bad men, as well as bad subjects." That is the way he reasoned. "I wish nothing but good, therefore every man who does not agree with me is a traitor and a scoundrel." Remember that he believed himself anointed by a Divine commission; remember that he was a man of slow parts and imperfect education; that the same awful will of Heaven which placed a crown upon his head, which made him tender to his family, pure in his life, courageous and honest, made him dull of comprehension, obstinate of will, and at many times deprived him of reason. He was the father of his people; his rebellious children must be flogged into obedience. He was the defender of the Protestant faith; he would rather lay that stout head upon the block than that Catholics should have a share in the government of England. And you do not suppose that there are not honest bigots enough in all countries to back kings in this kind of statesmanship? Without doubt the American war was popular in England. In 1775 the address in favour of coercing the colonies was carried by 304 to 105 in the Commons, by 104 to 29 in the House of Lords. Popular?—so was the Revocation of the Edict of Nantes popular in France: so was the massacre of St. Bartholomew: so was the Inquisition exceedingly popular in Spain.

Wars and revolutions are, however, the politician's province. The great events of this long reign, the statesmen and orators who illustrated it, I do not pretend to make the subjects of an hour's light talk.(187) Let us return to our humbler duty of Court gossip. Yonder sits our little queen, surrounded by many stout sons and fair daughters whom she bore to her faithful George. The history of the daughters, as little Miss Burney has painted them to us, is delightful. They were handsome—she calls them beautiful; they were most kind, loving, and ladylike; they were gracious to every person, high and low, who served them. They had many little accomplishments of their own. This one drew: that one played the piano: they all worked most prodigiously, and fitted up whole suites of rooms—pretty, smiling Penelopes,—with their busy little needles. As we picture to ourselves the society of eighty years ago, we must imagine hundreds of thousands of groups of women in great high caps, tight bodies, and full skirts, needling away, whilst one of the number, or perhaps a favoured gentleman in a pigtail, reads out a novel to the company. Peep into the cottage at Olney, for example, and see there Mrs. Unwin and Lady Hesketh, those high-bred ladies, those sweet, pious women, and William Cowper, that delicate wit, that trembling pietist, that refined gentleman, absolutely reading out Jonathan Wild to the ladies! What a change in our manners, in our amusements, since then!

King George's household was a model of an English gentleman's household. It was early; it was kindly; it was charitable; it was frugal; it was orderly; it must have been stupid to a degree which I shudder now to contemplate. No wonder all the princes ran away from the lap of that dreary domestic virtue. It always rose, rode, dined at stated intervals. Day after day was the same. At the same hour at night the king kissed his daughters' jolly cheeks; the princesses kissed their mother's hand; and Madame Thielke brought the royal nightcap. At the same hour the equerries and women in waiting had their little dinner, and cackled over their tea. The king had his backgammon or his evening concert; the equerries yawned themselves to death in the ante-room; or the king and his family walked on Windsor slopes, the king holding his darling little princess Amelia by the hand; and the people crowded round quite good-naturedly; and the Eton boys thrust their chubby cheeks under the crowd's elbows; and the concert over, the king never failed to take his enormous cocked-hat off, and salute his band, and say, "Thank you, gentlemen."

A quieter household, a more prosaic life than this of Kew or Windsor, cannot be imagined. Rain or shine, the king rode every day for hours; poked his red face into hundreds of cottages round about, and showed that shovel hat and Windsor uniform to farmers, to pig-boys, to old women making apple dumplings; to all sorts of people, gentle and simple, about whom countless stories are told. Nothing can be more undignified than these stories. When Haroun Alraschid visits a subject incog., the latter is sure to be very much the better for the caliph's magnificence. Old George showed no such royal splendour. He used to give a guinea sometimes: sometimes feel in his pockets and find he had no money: often ask a man a hundred questions: about the number of his family, about his oats and beans, about the rent he paid for his house, and ride on. On one occasion he played the part of King Alfred, and turned a piece of meat with a string at a cottager's house. When the old woman came home, she found a paper with an enclosure of money, and a note written by the royal pencil: "Five guineas to buy a jack." It was not splendid, but it was kind and worthy of Farmer George. One day, when the king and queen were walking together, they met a little boy—they were always fond of children, the good folks—and patted the little white head. "Whose little boy are you?" asks the Windsor uniform. "I am the king's beefeater's little boy," replied the child. On which the king said, "Then kneel down, and kiss the queen's hand." But the innocent offspring of the beefeater declined this treat. "No," said he, "I won't kneel, for if I do, I shall spoil my new breeches." The thrifty king ought to have hugged him and knighted him on the spot. George's admirers wrote pages and pages of such stories about him. One morning, before anybody else was up, the king walked about Gloucester town; pushed over Molly the housemaid who was scrubbing the doorsteps with her pail; ran upstairs and woke all the equerries in their bedrooms; and then trotted down to the bridge, where, by this time, a dozen of louts were assembled. "What! is this Gloucester New Bridge?" asked our gracious monarch; and the people answered him, "Yes, your Majesty." "Why, then, my boys," said he, "let us have a huzzay!" After giving them which intellectual gratification, he went home to breakfast. Our fathers read these simple tales with fond pleasure; laughed at these very small jokes; liked the old man who poked his nose into every cottage; who lived on plain wholesome roast and boiled; who despised your French kickshaws; who was a true hearty old English gentleman. You may have seen Gilray's famous print of him—in the old wig, in the stout old hideous Windsor uniform—as the King of Brobdingnag, peering at a little Gulliver, whom he holds up in his hand, whilst in the other he has an opera-glass, through which he surveys the pygmy? Our fathers chose to set up George as the type of a great king; and the little Gulliver was the great Napoleon. We prided ourselves on our prejudices; we blustered and bragged with absurd vainglory; we dealt to our enemy a monstrous injustice of contempt and scorn; we fought him with all weapons, mean as well as heroic. There was no lie we would not believe; no charge of crime which our furious prejudice would not credit. I thought at one time of making a collection of the lies which the French had written against us, and we had published against them during the war: it would be a strange memorial of popular falsehood.

Their majesties were very sociable potentates: and the Court Chronicler tells of numerous visits which they paid to their subjects, gentle and simple: with whom they dined; at whose great country-houses they stopped; or at whose poorer lodgings they affably partook of tea and bread-and-butter. Some of the great folks spent enormous sums in entertaining their sovereigns. As marks of special favour, the king and queen sometimes stood as sponsors for the children of the nobility. We find Lady Salisbury was so honoured in the year 1786; and in the year 1802, Lady Chesterfield. The Court News relates how her ladyship received their Majesties on a state bed "dressed with white satin and a profusion of lace: the counterpane of white satin embroidered with gold, and the bed of crimson satin lined with white". The child was first brought by the nurse to the Marchioness of Bath, who presided as chief nurse. Then the marchioness handed baby to the queen. Then the queen handed the little darling to the Bishop of Norwich, the officiating clergyman; and, the ceremony over, a cup of caudle was presented by the earl to his Majesty on one knee, on a large gold waiter, placed on a crimson velvet cushion. Misfortunes would occur in these interesting genuflectory ceremonies of royal worship. Bubb Dodington, Lord Melcombe, a very fat, puffy man, in a most gorgeous Court suit, had to kneel, Cumberland says, and was so fat and so tight that he could not get up again. "Kneel, sir, kneel!" cried my lord in waiting to a country mayor who had to read an address, but who went on with his compliment standing. "Kneel, sir, kneel!" cries my lord, in dreadful alarm. "I can't!" says the mayor, turning round; "don't you see I have got a wooden leg?" In the capital Burney Diary and Letters, the home and Court life of good old King George and good old Queen Charlotte are presented at portentous length. The king rose every morning at six: and had two hours to himself. He thought it effeminate to have a carpet in his bedroom. Shortly before eight, the queen and the royal family were always ready for him, and they proceeded to the king's chapel in the castle. There were no fires in the passages: the chapel was scarcely alight;

princesses, governesses, equerries grumbled and caught cold: but cold or hot, it was their duty to go: and, wet or dry, light or dark, the stout old George was always in his place to say Amen to the chaplain.

The queen's character is represented in Burney at full length. She was a sensible, most decorous woman; a very grand lady on state occasions, simple enough in ordinary life; well read as times went, and giving shrewd opinions about books; stingy, but not unjust; not generally unkind to her dependants, but invincible in her notions of etiquette, and quite angry if her people suffered ill-health in her service. She gave Miss Burney a shabby pittance, and led the poor young woman a life which well-nigh killed her. She never thought but that she was doing Burney the greatest favour, in taking her from freedom, fame, and competence, and killing her off with languor in that dreary Court. It was not dreary to her. Had she been servant instead of mistress, her spirit would never have broken down: she never would have put a pin out of place, or been a moment from her duty. She was not weak, and she could not pardon those who were. She was perfectly correct in life, and she hated poor sinners with a rancour such as virtue sometimes has. She must have had awful private trials of her own: not merely with her children, but with her husband, in those long days about which nobody will ever know anything now; when he was not quite insane; when his incessant tongue was babbling folly, rage, persecution; and she had to smile and be respectful and attentive under this intolerable ennui. The queen bore all her duties stoutly, as she expected others to bear them. At a state christening, the lady who held the infant was tired and looked unwell, and the Princess of Wales asked permission for her to sit down. "Let her stand," said the queen, flicking the snuff off her sleeve. She would have stood, the resolute old woman, if she had had to hold the child till his beard was grown. "I am seventy years of age," the queen said, facing a mob of ruffians who stopped her sedan: "I have been fifty years Queen of England, and I never was insulted before." Fearless, rigid, unforgiving little queen! I don't wonder that her sons revolted from her.

Of all the figures in that large family group which surrounds George and his queen, the prettiest, I think, is the father's darling, the Princess Amelia, pathetic for her beauty, her sweetness, her early death, and for the extreme passionate tenderness with which her father loved her. This was his favourite amongst all the children: of his sons, he loved the Duke of York best. Burney tells a sad story of the poor old man at Weymouth, and how eager he was to have this darling son with him. The king's house was not big enough to hold the prince; and his father had a portable house erected close to his own, and at huge pains, so that his dear Frederick should be near him. He clung on his arm all the time of his visit: talked to no one else; had talked of no one else for some time before. The prince, so long expected, stayed but a single night. He had business in London the next day, he said. The dullness of the old king's Court stupefied York and the other big sons of George III. They scared equerries and ladies, frightened the modest little circle, with their coarse spirits and loud talk. Of little comfort, indeed, were the king's sons to the king.

But the pretty Amelia was his darling; and the little maiden, prattling and smiling in the fond arms of that old father, is a sweet image to look on. There is a family picture in Burney, which a man must be very hard-hearted not to like. She describes an after-dinner walk of the royal family at Windsor:—"It was really a mighty pretty procession," she says. "The little princess, just turned of three years old, in a robe-coat covered with fine muslin, a dressed close cap, white gloves, and fan, walked on alone and first, highly delighted with the parade, and turning from side to side to see everybody as she passed; for all the terracers stand up against the walls, to make a clear passage for the royal family the moment they come in sight. Then followed the king and queen, no less delighted with the joy of their little darling. The Princess Royal leaning on Lady Elizabeth Waldegrave, the Princess Augusta holding by the Duchess of Ancaster, the Princess Elizabeth led by Lady Charlotte Bertie, followed. Office here takes place of rank," says Burney,—to explain how it was that Lady E. Waldegrave, as lady of the bed-chamber, walked before a duchess;—"General Budé, and the Duke of Montague, and Major Price as equerry, brought up the rear of the procession." One sees it; the band playing its old music, the sun shining on the happy, loyal crowd; and lighting the ancient battlements, the rich elms, and purple landscape, and bright greensward; the royal standard drooping from the great tower yonder; as old George passes, followed by his race, preceded by the charming infant, who caresses the crowd with her innocent smiles.

"On sight of Mrs. Delany, the king instantly stopped to speak to her; the queen, of course, and the little princess, and all the rest, stood still. They talked a good while with the sweet old lady, during which time the king once or twice addressed himself to me. I caught the queen's eye, and saw in it a little surprise, but by no means any displeasure, to see me of the party. The little princess went up to Mrs. Delany, of whom she is very fond, and behaved like a little angel to her. She then, with a look of inquiry and recollection, came behind Mrs. Delany to look at me. 'I am afraid,' said I, in a whisper, and stooping down, 'your Royal Highness does not remember me?' Her answer was an arch little smile, and a nearer approach, with her lips pouted out to kiss me."

The princess wrote verses herself, and there are some pretty plaintive lines attributed to her, which are more touching than better poetry:—

Unthinking, idle, wild, and young,
I laughed, and danced, and talked, and sung:
And, proud of health, of freedom vain,
Dreamed not of sorrow, care, or pain:
Concluding, in those hours of glee,
That all the world was made for me.

But when the hour of trial came,
When sickness shook this trembling frame,
When folly's gay pursuits were o'er,
And I could sing and dance no more,
It then occurred, how sad 'twould be
Were this world only made for me.

The poor soul quitted it—and ere yet she was dead the agonized father was in such a state, that the officers round about him were obliged to set watchers over him, and from November, 1810, George III ceased to reign. All the world knows the story of his malady: all history presents no sadder figure than that of the old man, blind and deprived of reason, wandering through the rooms of his palace, addressing imaginary Parliaments, reviewing fancied troops, holding ghostly Courts. I have seen his picture as it was taken at this time, hanging in the apartment of his daughter, the Landgravine of Hesse-Hombourg—amidst books and Windsor furniture, and a hundred fond reminiscences of her English home. The poor old father is represented in a purple gown, his snowy beard falling over his breast—the star of his famous Order still idly shining on it. He was not only sightless: he became utterly deaf. All light, all reason, all sound of human voices, all the pleasures of this world of God, were taken from him. Some slight lucid moments he had; in one of which, the queen, desiring to see him, entered the room, and found him singing a hymn, and accompanying himself at the harpsichord. When he had finished, he knelt down and prayed aloud for her, and then for his family, and then for the nation, concluding with a prayer for himself, that it might please God to avert his heavy calamity from him, but if not, to give him resignation to submit. He then burst into tears, and his reason again fled.

What preacher need moralize on this story; what words save the simplest are requisite to tell it? It is too terrible for tears. The thought of such a misery smites me down in submission before the Ruler of kings and men, the Monarch Supreme over empires and republics, the inscrutable Dispenser of life, death, happiness, victory. "O brothers," I said to those who heard me first in America—"O brothers! speaking the same dear mother tongue—O comrades! enemies no more, let us take a mournful hand together as we stand by this royal corpse, and call a truce to battle! Low he lies to whom the proudest used to kneel once, and who was cast lower than the poorest: dead, whom millions prayed for in vain. Driven off his throne; buffeted by rude hands; with his children in revolt; the darling of his old age killed before him untimely; our Lear hangs over her breathless lips and cries, 'Cordelia, Cordelia, stay a little!'"

Vex not his ghost—oh! let him pass—he hates him
That would upon the rack of this tough world
Stretch him out longer!

Hush, Strife and Quarrel, over the solemn grave! Sound, trumpets, a mournful march! Fall, dark curtain, upon his pageant, his pride, his grief, his awful tragedy!

George The Fourth

In Twiss's amusing Life of Eldon, we read how, on the death of the Duke of York, the old chancellor became possessed of a lock of the defunct prince's hair; and so careful was he respecting the authenticity of the relic, that Bessy Eldon his wife sat in the room with the young man from Hamlet's, who distributed the ringlet into separate lockets, which each of the Eldon family afterwards wore. You know how, when George IV came to Edinburgh, a better man than he went on board the royal yacht to welcome the king to his kingdom of Scotland, seized a goblet from which his majesty had just drunk, vowed it should remain for ever as an heirloom in his family, clapped the precious glass in his pocket, and sat down on it and broke it when he got home. Suppose the good sheriff's prize unbroken now at Abbotsford, should we not smile with something like pity as we beheld it? Suppose one of those lockets of the No-Popery prince's hair offered for sale at Christie's, quot libras e duce summo invenies? how many pounds would you find for the illustrious duke? Madame Tussaud has got King George's coronation robes; is there any man now alive who would kiss the hem of that trumpery? He sleeps since thirty years: do not any of you, who remember him, wonder that you once respected and huzza'd and admired him?

To make a portrait of him at first seemed a matter of small difficulty. There is his coat, his star, his wig, his countenance simpering under it: with a slate and a piece of chalk, I could at this very desk perform a recognizable likeness of him. And yet after reading of him in scores of volumes, hunting him through old magazines and newspapers, having him here at a ball, there at a public dinner, there at races and so forth, you find you have nothing—nothing but a coat and wig and a mask smiling below it—nothing but a great simulacrum. His sire and grandsires were men. One knows what they were like: what they would do in given circumstances: that on occasion they fought and demeaned themselves like tough good soldiers. They had friends whom they liked according to their natures; enemies whom they hated fiercely; passions, and actions, and individualities of their own. The sailor king who came after George was a man: the Duke of York was a man, big, burly, loud, jolly, cursing, courageous. But this George, what was he? I look through all his life, and recognize but a bow and a grin. I try and take him to pieces, and find silk stockings, padding, stays, a coat with frogs and a fur collar, a star and blue ribbon, a pocket-handkerchief prodigiously scented, one of Truefitt's best nutty brown wigs reeking with oil, a set of teeth and a huge black stock, under-waistcoats, more under-waistcoats, and then nothing. I know of no sentiment that he ever distinctly uttered. Documents are published under his name, but people wrote them—private letters, but people spelt them. He put a great "George P." or "George R." at the bottom of the page and fancied he had written the paper: some bookseller's clerk, some poor author, some man did the work; saw to the spelling, cleaned up the slovenly sentences, and gave the lax maudlin slipslop a sort of consistency. He must have had an individuality: the dancing-master whom he emulated, nay, surpassed—the wig-maker who curled his toupee for him—the tailor who cut his coats, had that. But, about George, one can get at nothing actual. That outside, I am certain, is pad and tailor's work; there may be something behind, but what? We cannot get at the character; no doubt never shall. Will men of the future have nothing better to do than to unswathe and interpret that royal old mummy? I own I once used to think it would be good sport to pursue him, fasten on him, and pull him down. But now I am ashamed to mount and lay good dogs on, to summon a full field, and then to hunt the poor game.

On the 12th August, 1762, the forty-seventh anniversary of the accession of the House of Brunswick to the English throne, all the bells in London pealed in gratulation, and announced that an heir to George III was born. Five days afterwards the king was pleased to pass letters patent under the great seal, creating H.R.H. the Prince of Great Britain, Electoral Prince of Brunswick-Lüneburg, Duke of Cornwall and Rothsay, Earl of Carrick, Baron of Renfrew, Lord of the Isles, and Great Steward of Scotland, Prince of Wales and Earl of Chester.

All the people at his birth thronged to see this lovely child; and behind a gilt china-screen railing in St. James's Palace, in a cradle surmounted by the three princely ostrich feathers, the royal infant was laid to delight the eyes of the lieges. Among the earliest instances of homage paid to him, I read that "a curious Indian bow and arrows were sent to the prince from his father's faithful subjects in New York". He was fond of playing with these toys: an old statesman, orator, and wit of his grandfather's and great-grandfather's time, never tired of his business, still eager in his old age to be well at Court, used to play with the little prince, and pretend to fall down dead when the prince shot at him with his toy bow and arrows—and get up and fall down dead over and over again—to the increased delight of the child. So that he was flattered from his cradle upwards; and before his little feet could walk, statesmen and courtiers were busy kissing them.

There is a pretty picture of the royal infant—a beautiful buxom child—asleep in his mother's lap; who turns round and holds a finger to her lip, as if she would bid the courtiers around respect the baby's slumbers. From that day until his decease, sixty-eight years after, I suppose there were more pictures taken of that personage than of any other human being who ever was born and died—in every kind of uniform and every possible Court dress—in long fair hair, with powder, with and without a pigtail—in every conceivable cocked-hat—in dragoon uniform—in Windsor uniform—in a field-marshal's clothes—in a Scotch kilt and tartans, with dirk and claymore (a stupendous figure)—in a frogged frock-coat with a fur collar and tight breeches and silk stockings—in wigs of every colour, fair, brown, and black—in his famous coronation robes finally, with which performance he was so much in love that he distributed copies of the picture to all the Courts and British embassies in Europe, and to numberless clubs, town-halls, and private friends. I remember as a young man how almost every dining-room had his portrait.

There is plenty of biographical tattle about the prince's boyhood. It is told with what astonishing rapidity he learned all languages, ancient and modern; how he rode beautifully, sang charmingly, and played elegantly on the violoncello. That he was beautiful was patent to all eyes. He had a high spirit: and once, when he had had a difference with his father, burst into the royal closet and called out, "Wilkes and liberty for ever!" He was so clever, that he confounded his very governors in learning; and one of them, Lord Bruce, having made a false quantity in quoting Greek, the admirable young prince instantly corrected him. Lord Bruce could not remain a governor after this humiliation; resigned his office, and, to soothe his feelings, was actually promoted to be an earl! It is the most wonderful reason for promoting a man that ever I heard. Lord Bruce was made an earl for a blunder in prosody; and Nelson was made a baron for the victory of the Nile.

Lovers of long sums have added up the millions and millions which in the course of his brilliant existence this single prince consumed. Besides his income of 50,000 l., 70,000 l., 100,000 l., 120,000 l. a year, we read of three applications to Parliament: debts to the amount of 160,000 l., of 650,000 l.; besides mysterious foreign loans, whereof he pocketed the proceeds. What did he do for all this money? Why was he to have it? If he had been a manufacturing town, or a populous rural district, or an army of five thousand men, he would not have cost more. He, one solitary stout man, who did not toil, nor spin, nor fight,—what had any mortal done that he should be pampered so?

In 1784, when he was twenty-one years of age, Carlton Palace was given to him, and furnished by the nation with as much luxury as could be devised. His pockets were filled with money: he said it was not enough; he flung it out of window: he spent 10,000 l. a year for the coats on his back. The nation gave him more money, and more, and more. The sum is past counting. He was a prince, most lovely to look on, and christened Prince Florizel on his first appearance in the world. That he was the handsomest prince in the whole world was agreed by men, and alas! by many women.

I suppose he must have been very graceful. There are so many testimonies to the charm of his manner, that we must allow him great elegance and powers of fascination. He, and the King of France's brother, the Count d'Artois, a charming young prince who danced deliciously on the tight-rope—a poor old tottering exiled king, who asked hospitality of King George's successor, and lived awhile in the palace of Mary Stuart—divided in their youth the title of first gentleman of Europe. We in England of course gave the prize to our gentleman. Until George's death the propriety of that award was scarce questioned or the doubters voted rebels and traitors. Only the other day I was reading in the reprint of the delightful Noctes of Christopher North. The health of THE KING is drunk in large capitals by the loyal Scotsman. You would fancy him a hero, a sage, a statesman, a pattern for kings and men. It was Walter Scott who had that accident with the broken glass I spoke of anon. He was the king's Scottish champion, rallied all Scotland to him, made loyalty the fashion, and laid about him fiercely with his claymore upon all the prince's enemies. The Brunswicks had no such defenders as those two Jacobite commoners, old Sam Johnson the Lichfield chapman's son, and Walter Scott, the Edinburgh lawyer's.

Nature and circumstance had done their utmost to prepare the prince for being spoiled: the dreadful dullness of papa's Court, its stupid amusements, its dreary occupations, the maddening humdrum, the stifling sobriety of its routine, would have made a scapegrace of a much less lively prince. All the big princes bolted from that castle of ennui where old King George sat, posting up his books and droning over his Handel; and old Queen Charlotte over her snuff and her tambour-frame. Most of the sturdy, gallant sons settled down after sowing their wild oats, and became sober subjects of their father and brother—not ill liked by the nation, which pardons youthful irregularities readily enough, for the sake of pluck, and unaffectedness, and good humour.

The boy is father of the man. Our prince signalized his entrance into the world by a feat worthy of his future life. He invented a new shoebuckle. It was an inch long and five inches broad. "It covered almost the whole instep, reaching down to the ground on either side of the foot." A sweet invention! lovely and useful as the prince on whose foot it sparkled. At his first appearance at a Court ball, we read that "his coat was pink silk, with white cuffs; his waistcoat white silk, embroidered with various-coloured foil, and adorned with a profusion of French paste. And his hat was ornamented with two rows of steel beads, five thousand in number, with a button and loop of the same metal, and cocked in a new military style". What a Florizel! Do these details seem trivial? They are the grave incidents of his life. His biographers say that when he commenced housekeeping in that splendid new palace of his, the Prince of Wales had some windy projects of encouraging literature, science, and the arts; of having assemblies of literary characters; and societies for the encouragement of geography, astronomy, and botany. Astronomy, geography, and botany! Fiddlesticks! French ballet-dancers, French cooks, horse-jockeys, buffoons, procurers, tailors, boxers, fencing-masters, china, jewel, and gimcrack merchants—these were his real companions. At first he made a pretence of having Burke and Pitt and Sheridan for his friends. But how could such men be serious before such an empty scapegrace as this lad? Fox might talk dice with him, and Sheridan wine; but what else had these men of genius in common with their tawdry young host of Carlton House? That ribble the leader of such men as Fox and Burke! That man's opinions about the constitution, the India Bill, justice to the Catholics—about any question graver than the button for a waistcoat or the sauce for a partridge—worth anything! The friendship between the prince and the Whig chiefs was impossible. They were hypocrites in pretending to respect him, and if he broke the hollow compact between them, who shall blame him? His natural companions were dandies and parasites. He could talk to a tailor or a cook; but, as the equal of great statesmen, to set up a creature, lazy, weak, indolent, besotted, of monstrous vanity, and levity incurable—it is absurd. They thought to use him, and did for awhile; but they must have known how timid he was; how entirely heartless and treacherous, and have expected his desertion. His next set of friends were mere table companions, of whom he grew tired too; then we hear of him with a very few select toadies, mere boys from school or the Guards, whose sprightliness tickled the fancy of the worn-out voluptuary. What matters what friends he had? He dropped all his friends; he never could have real friends. An heir to the throne has flatterers, adventurers who hang about him, ambitious men who use him; but friendship is denied him.

And women, I suppose, are as false and selfish in their dealings with such a character as men. Shall we take the Leporello part, flourish a catalogue of the conquests of this royal Don Juan, and tell the names of the favourites to whom, one after the other, George Prince flung his pocket-handkerchief? What purpose would it answer to say how Perdita was pursued, won, deserted, and by whom succeeded? What good in knowing that he did actually marry Mrs. FitzHerbert according to the rites of the Roman Catholic Church; that her marriage settlements have been seen in London; that the names of the witnesses to her marriage are known. This sort of vice that we are now come to presents no new or fleeting trait of manners. Debauchees, dissolute, heartless, fickle, cowardly, have been ever since the world began. This one had more temptations than most, and so much may be said in extenuation for him.

It was an unlucky thing for this doomed one, and tending to lead him yet farther on the road to the deuce, that, besides being lovely, so that women were fascinated by him; and heir apparent, so that all the world flattered him; he should have a beautiful voice, which led him directly in the way of drink: and thus all the pleasant devils were coaxing on poor Florizel; desire, and idleness, and vanity, and drunkenness, all clashing their merry cymbals and bidding him come on.

We first hear of his warbling sentimental ditties under the walls of Kew Palace by the moonlight banks of Thames, with Lord Viscount Leporello keeping watch lest the music should be disturbed.

Singing after dinner and supper was the universal fashion of the day. You may fancy all England sounding with choruses, some ribald, some harmless, but all occasioning the consumption of a prodigious deal of fermented liquor.

The jolly Muse her wings to try no frolic flights need take,
But round the bowl would dip and fly, like swallows round a lake,

sang Morris in one of his gallant Anacreontics, to which the prince many a time joined in chorus, and of which the burden is,—

And that I think's a reason fair to drink and fill again.

This delightful boon companion of the prince's found "a reason fair" to forgo filling and drinking, saw the error of his ways, gave up the bowl and chorus, and died retired and religious. The prince's table no doubt was a very tempting one. The wits came and did their utmost to amuse him. It is wonderful how the spirits rise, the wit brightens, the wine has an aroma, when a great man is at the head of the table. Scott, the loyal cavalier, the king's true liegeman, the very best raconteur of his time, poured out with an endless generosity his store of old-world learning, kindness, and humour. Grattan contributed to it his wondrous eloquence, fancy, feeling. Tom Moore perched upon it for awhile, and piped his most exquisite little love-tunes on it, flying away in a twitter of indignation afterwards, and attacking the prince with bill and claw. In such society, no wonder the sitting was long, and the butler tired of drawing corks. Remember what the usages of the time were, and that William Pitt, coming to the House of Commons after having drunk a bottle of port wine at his own house, would go into Bellamy's with Dundas, and help finish a couple more.

You peruse volumes after volumes about our prince, and find some half-dozen stock stories—indeed not many more—common to all the histories. He was good-natured; an indolent, voluptuous prince, not unkindly. One story, the most favourable to him of all, perhaps, is that as Prince Regent he was eager to hear all that could be said in behalf of prisoners condemned to death, and anxious, if possible, to remit the capital sentence. He was kind to his servants. There is a story common to all the biographies, of Molly the housemaid, who, when his household was to be broken up, owing to some reforms which he tried absurdly to practise, was discovered crying as she dusted the chairs because she was to leave a master who had a kind word for all his servants. Another tale is that of a groom of the prince's being discovered in corn and oat peculations, and dismissed by the personage at the head of the stables; the prince had word of John's disgrace, remonstrated with him very kindly, generously reinstated him, and bade him promise to sin no more—a promise which John kept. Another story is very fondly told of the prince as a young man hearing of an officer's family in distress, and how he straightway borrowed six or eight hundred pounds, put his long fair hair under his hat, and so disguised carried the money to the starving family. He sent money, too, to Sheridan on his death-bed, and would have sent more had not death ended the career of that man of genius. Besides these, there are a few pretty speeches, kind and graceful, to persons with whom he was brought in contact. But he turned upon twenty friends. He was fond and familiar with them one day, and he passed them on the next without recognition. He used them, liked them, loved them perhaps in his way, and then separated from them. On Monday he kissed and fondled poor Perdita, and on Tuesday he met her and did not know her. On Wednesday he was very affectionate with that wretched Brummell, and on Thursday forgot him; cheated him even out of a snuff-box which he owed the poor dandy; saw him years afterwards in his downfall and poverty, when the bankrupt Beau sent him another snuff-box with some of the snuff he used to love, as a piteous token of remembrance and submission, and the king took the snuff, and ordered his horses and drove on, and had not the grace to notice his old companion, favourite, rival, enemy, superior. In Wraxall there is some gossip about him. When the charming, beautiful, generous Duchess of Devonshire died—the lovely lady whom he used to call his dearest duchess once, and pretend to admire as all English society admired her—he said, "Then we have lost the best-bred woman in England." "Then we have lost the kindest heart in England," said noble Charles Fox. On another occasion, when three noblemen were to receive the Garter, says Wraxall, "a great personage observed that never did three men receive the order in so characteristic a manner. The Duke of A. advanced to the sovereign with a phlegmatic, cold, awkward air like a clown; Lord B. came forward fawning and smiling like a courtier; Lord C. presented himself easy, unembarrassed, like a gentleman!" These are the stories one has to recall about the prince and king—kindness to a housemaid, generosity to a groom, criticism on a bow. There are no better stories about him: they are mean and trivial, and they characterize him. The great war of empires and giants goes on. Day by day victories are won and lost by the brave. Torn, smoky flags and battered eagles are wrenched from the heroic enemy and laid at his feet; and he sits there on his throne and smiles, and gives the guerdon of valour to the conqueror. He! Elliston the actor, when the Coronation was performed, in which he took the principal part, used to fancy himself the king, burst into tears, and hiccup a blessing on the people. I believe it is certain about George IV, that he had heard so much of the war, knighted so many people, and worn such a prodigious quantity of marshal's uniforms, cocked-hats, cock's feathers, scarlet and bullion in general, that he actually fancied he had been present in some campaigns, and, under the name of General Brock, led a tremendous charge of the German legion at Waterloo.

He is dead but thirty years, and one asks how a great society could have tolerated him? Would we bear him now? In this quarter of a century, what a silent revolution has been working! how it has separated us from old times and manners! How it has changed men themselves! I can see old gentlemen now among us, of perfect good breeding, of quiet lives, with venerable grey heads, fondling their grandchildren; and look at them, and wonder at what they were once. That gentleman of the grand old school, when he was in the 10th Hussars, and dined at the prince's table, would fall under it night after night. Night after night, that gentleman sat at Brookes's or Raggett's over the dice. If, in the petulance of play or drink, that gentleman spoke a sharp word to his neighbour, he and the other would infallibly go out and try to shoot each other the next morning. That gentleman would drive his friend Richmond the black boxer down to Moulsey, and hold his coat, and shout and swear, and hurrah with delight, whilst the black man was beating Dutch Sam the Jew. That gentleman would take a manly pleasure in pulling his own coat off, and thrashing a bargeman in a street row. That gentleman has been in a watchhouse. That gentleman, so exquisitely polite with ladies in a drawing-room, so loftily courteous, if he talked now as he used among men in his youth, would swear so as to make your hair stand on end. I met lately a very old German gentleman, who had served in our army at the beginning of the century. Since then he has lived on his own estate, but rarely meeting with an Englishman, whose language—the language of fifty years ago that is—he possesses perfectly. When this highly bred old man began to speak English to me, almost every other word he uttered was an oath: as they used it (they swore dreadfully in Flanders) with the Duke of York before Valenciennes, or at Carlton House over the supper and cards. Read Byron's letters. So accustomed is the young man to oaths that he employs them even in writing to his friends, and swears by the post. Read his account of the doings of young men at Cambridge, of the ribald professors, one of whom "could pour out Greek like a drunken helot", and whose excesses surpassed even those of the young men. Read Matthews's description of the boyish lordling's housekeeping at Newstead, the skull-cup passed round, the monks' dresses from the masquerade warehouse, in which the young scapegraces used to sit until daylight, chanting appropriate songs round their wine. "We come to breakfast at two or three o'clock," Matthews says. "There are gloves and foils for those who like to amuse themselves, or we fire pistols at a mark in the hall, or we worry the wolf." A jolly life truly! The noble young owner of the mansion writes about such affairs himself in letters to his friend, Mr. John Jackson, pugilist, in London.

All the prince's time tells a similar strange story of manners and pleasure. In Wraxall we find the prime minister himself, the redoubted William Pitt, engaged in high jinks with personages of no less importance than Lord Thurlow the lord chancellor, and Mr. Dundas the treasurer of the navy. Wraxall relates how these three statesmen, returning after dinner from Addiscombe, found a turnpike open and galloped through it without paying the toll. The turnpike man, fancying they were highwaymen, fired a blunderbuss after them, but missed them; and the poet sang,—

How as Pitt wandered darkling o'er the plain,
His reason drown'd in Jenkinson's champagne,
A rustic's hand, but righteous fate withstood,
Had shed a premier's for a robber's blood.

Here we have the treasurer of the navy, the lord high chancellor, and the prime minister, all engaged in a most undoubted lark. In Eldon's Memoirs, about the very same time, I read that the Bar loved wine, as well as the woolsack. Not John Scott himself; he was a good boy always; and though he loved port wine, loved his business and his duty and his fees a great deal better.

He has a Northern Circuit story of those days, about a party at the house of a certain Lawyer Fawcett, who gave a dinner every year to the counsel.

"On one occasion," related Lord Eldon, "I heard Lee say, 'I cannot leave Fawcett's wine. Mind, Davenport, you will go home immediately after dinner, to read the brief in that cause that we have to conduct to-morrow.'

"'Not I,' said Davenport. 'Leave my dinner and my wine to read a brief! No, no, Lee; that won't do.'

"'Then,' said Lee, 'what is to be done? who else is employed?'

"Davenport.—'Oh! young Scott.'

"Lee.—'Oh! he must go. Mr. Scott, you must go home immediately, and make yourself acquainted with that cause, before our consultation this evening.'"

"This was very hard upon me; but I did go, and there was an attorney from Cumberland, and one from Northumberland, and I do not know how many other persons. Pretty late, in came Jack Lee, as drunk as he could be.

"'I cannot consult to-night; I must go to bed,' he exclaimed, and away he went. Then came Sir Thomas Davenport.

"'We cannot have a consultation to-night, Mr. Wordsworth' (Wordsworth, I think, was the name; it was a Cumberland name), shouted Davenport. 'Don't you see how drunk Mr. Scott is? it is impossible to consult.' Poor me! who had scarce had any dinner, and lost all my wine—I was so drunk that I could not consult! Well, a verdict was given against us, and it was all owing to Lawyer Fawcett's dinner. We moved for a new trial; and I must say, for the honour of the Bar, that those two gentlemen, Jack Lee and Sir Thomas Davenport, paid all the expenses between them of the first trial. It is the only instance I ever knew, but they did. We moved for a new trial (on the ground, I suppose, of the counsel not being in their senses), and it was granted. When it came on, the following year, the judge rose and said,—

"'Gentlemen, did any of you dine with Lawyer Fawcett yesterday? for, if you did, I will not hear this cause till next year.'

"There was great laughter. We gained the cause that time."

On another occasion, at Lancaster, where poor Bozzy must needs be going the Northern Circuit, "we found him," says Mr. Scott, "lying upon the pavement inebriated. We subscribed a guinea at supper for him, and a half-crown for his clerk"—(no doubt there was a large Bar, and that Scott's joke did not cost him much),—"and sent him, when he waked next morning, a brief, with instructions to move for what we denominated the writ of quare adhaesit pavimento? with observations duly calculated to induce him to think that it required great learning to explain the necessity of granting it, to the judge before whom he was to move." Boswell sent all round the town to attorneys for books, that might enable him to distinguish himself—but in vain. He moved, however, for the writ, making the best use he could of the observations in the brief. The judge was perfectly astonished, and the audience amazed. The judge said, "I never heard of such a writ—what can it be that adheres pavimento? Are any of you gentlemen at the Bar able to explain this?"

The Bar laughed. At last one of them said,—

"My lord, Mr. Boswell last night adhaesit pavimento. There was no moving him for some time. At last he was carried to bed, and he has been dreaming about himself and the pavement."

The canny old gentleman relishes these jokes. When the Bishop of Lincoln was moving from the deanery of St. Paul's, he says he asked a learned friend of his, by name Will Hay, how he should move some especially fine claret, about which he was anxious.

"Pray, my lord bishop," says Hay, "how much of the wine have you?"

The bishop said six dozen.

"If that is all," Hay answered, "you have but to ask me six times to dinner, and I will carry it all away myself."

There were giants in those days; but this joke about wine is not so fearful as one perpetrated by Orator Thelwall, in the heat of the French Revolution, ten years later, over a frothing pot of porter. He blew the head off, and said, "This is the way I would serve all kings."

Now we come to yet higher personages, and find their doings recorded in the blushing pages of timid little Miss Burney's Memoirs. She represents a prince of the blood in quite a royal condition. The loudness, the bigness, boisterousness, creaking boots and rattling oaths, of the young princes, appeared to have frightened the prim household of Windsor, and set all the tea-cups twittering on the tray. On the night of a ball and birthday, when one of the pretty, kind princesses was to come out, it was agreed that her brother, Prince William Henry, should dance the opening minuet with her, and he came to visit the household at their dinner.

"At dinner, Mrs. Schwellenberg presided, attired magnificently; Miss Goldsworthy, Mrs. Stanforth, Messrs. Du Luc and Stanhope, dined with us; and while we were still eating fruit, the Duke of Clarence entered.

"He was just risen from the king's table, and waiting for his equipage to go home and prepare for the ball. To give you an idea of the energy of his royal highness's language, I ought to set apart an objection to writing, or rather intimating, certain forcible words, and beg leave to show you in genuine colours a royal sailor.

"We all rose, of course, upon his entrance, and the two gentlemen placed themselves behind their chairs, while the footmen left the room. But he ordered us all to sit down, and called the men back to hand about some wine. He was in exceeding high spirits, and in the utmost good humour. He placed himself at the head of the table, next Mrs. Schwellenberg, and looked remarkably well, gay, and full of sport and mischief; yet clever withal, as well as comical.

"'Well, this is the first day I have ever dined with the king at St. James's on his birthday. Pray, have you all drunk his majesty's health?'

"'No, your royal highness; your royal highness might make dem do dat,' said Mrs. Schwellenberg.

"'Oh, by —, I will! Here, you' (to the footman). 'bring champagne; I'll drink the king's health again, if I die for it. Yes, I have done it pretty well already; so has the king, I promise you! I believe his majesty was never taken such good care of before; we have kept his spirits up, I promise you; we have enabled him to go through his fatigues; and I should have done more still, but for the ball and Mary;—I have promised to dance with Mary. I must keep sober for Mary.'"

Indefatigable Miss Burney continues for a dozen pages reporting H.R.H.'s conversation, and indicating, with a humour not unworthy of the clever little author of Evelina, the increasing state of excitement of the young sailor prince, who drank more and more champagne, stopped old Mrs. Schwellenberg's remonstrances by giving the old lady a kiss, and telling her to hold her potato-trap, and who did not "keep sober for Mary". Mary had to find another partner that night, for the royal William Henry could not keep his legs.

Will you have a picture of the amusements of another royal prince? It is the Duke of York, the blundering general, the beloved commander-in-chief of the army, the brother with whom George IV had had many a midnight carouse, and who continued his habits of pleasure almost till death seized his stout body.

In Pückler Muskau's Letters, that German prince describes a bout with H.R.H., who in his best time was such a powerful toper that "six bottles of claret after dinner scarce made a perceptible change in his countenance".

"I remember," says Pückler, "that one evening,—indeed, it was past midnight,—he took some of his guests, among whom were the Austrian ambassador, Count Meervelt, Count Beroldingen, and myself, into his beautiful armoury. We tried to swing several Turkish sabres, but none of us had a very firm grasp; whence it happened that the duke and Meervelt both scratched themselves with a sort of straight Indian sword so as to draw blood. Meervelt then wished to try if the sword cut as well as a Damascus, and attempted to cut through one of the wax candles that stood on the table. The experiment answered so ill, that both the candles, candlesticks and all, fell to the ground and were extinguished. While we were groping in the dark and trying to find the door, the duke's aide de camp stammered out in great agitation, 'By G—, sir, I remember the sword is poisoned.!'

"You may conceive the agreeable feelings of the wounded at this intelligence! Happily, on further examination, it appeared that claret, and not poison, was at the bottom of the colonel's exclamation."

And now I have one more story of the bacchanalian sort, in which Clarence and York, and the very highest personage of the realm, the great Prince Regent, all play parts. The feast took place at the Pavilion at Brighton, and was described to me by a gentleman who was present at the scene. In Gilray's caricatures, and amongst Fox's jolly associates, there figures a great nobleman, the Duke of Norfolk, called Jockey of Norfolk in his time, and celebrated for his table exploits. He had quarrelled with the prince, like the rest of the Whigs; but a sort of reconciliation had taken place; and now, being a very old man, the prince invited him to dine and sleep at the Pavilion, and the old duke drove over from his castle of Arundel with his famous equipage of grey horses, still remembered in Sussex.

The Prince of Wales had concocted with his royal brothers a notable scheme for making the old man drunk. Every person at table was enjoined to drink wine with the duke—a challenge which the old toper did not refuse. He soon began to see that there was a conspiracy against him; he drank glass for glass; he overthrew many of the brave. At last the First Gentleman of Europe proposed bumpers of brandy. One of the royal brothers filled a great glass for the duke. He stood up and tossed off the drink. "Now," says he, "I will have my carriage, and go home." The prince urged upon him his previous promise to sleep under the roof where he had been so generously entertained. "No," he said, he had had enough of such hospitality. A trap had been set for him; he would leave the place at once and never enter its doors more.

The carriage was called, and came; but, in the half-hour's interval, the liquor had proved too potent for the old man; his host's generous purpose was answered, and the duke's old grey head lay stupefied on the table. Nevertheless, when his post-chaise was announced, he staggered to it as well as he could, and stumbling in, bade the postilions drive to Arundel. They drove him for half an hour round and round the Pavilion lawn; the poor old man fancied he was going home. When he awoke that morning he was in bed at the prince's hideous house at Brighton. You may see the place now for sixpence: they have fiddlers there every day; and sometimes buffoons and mountebanks hire the Riding House and do their tricks and tumbling there. The trees are still there, and the gravel walks round which the poor old sinner was trotted. I can fancy the flushed faces of the royal princes as they support themselves at the portico pillars, and look on at old Norfolk's disgrace; but I can't fancy how the man who perpetrated it continued to be called a gentleman.

From drinking, the pleased Muse now turns to gambling, of which in his youth our prince was a great practitioner. He was a famous pigeon for the play-men; they lived upon him. Egalité Orleans, it was believed, punished him severely. A noble lord, whom we shall call the Marquis of Steyne, is said to have mulcted him in immense sums. He frequented the clubs, where play was then almost universal; and, as it was known his debts of honour were sacred, whilst he was gambling Jews waited outside to purchase his notes of hand. His transactions on the turf were unlucky as well as discreditable: though I believe he, and his jockey, and his horse Escape, were all innocent in that affair which created so much scandal.

Arthur's, Almack's, Bootle's, and White's were the chief clubs of the young men of fashion. There was play at all, and decayed noblemen and broken-down senators fleeced the unwary there. In Selwyn's Letters we find Carlisle, Devonshire, Coventry, Queensberry, all undergoing the probation. Charles Fox, a dreadful gambler, was cheated in very late times—lost 200,000 l. at play. Gibbon tells of his playing for twenty-two hours at a sitting, and losing 500 l. an hour. That indomitable punter said that the greatest pleasure in life, after winning, was losing. What hours, what nights, what health did he waste over the devil's books! I was going to say what peace of mind; but he took his losses very philosophically. After an awful night's play, and the enjoyment of the greatest pleasure but one in life, he was found on a sofa tranquilly reading an Eclogue of Virgil.

Play survived long after the wild prince and Fox had given up the dice-box. The dandies continued it. Byron, Brummell—how many names could I mention of men of the world who have suffered by it! In 1837 occurred a famous trial which pretty nigh put an end to gambling in England. A peer of the realm was found cheating at whist, and repeatedly seen to practise the trick called sauter la coupe. His friends at the clubs saw him cheat, and went on playing with him. One greenhorn, who had discovered his foul play, asked an old hand what he should do. "Do!" said the Mammon of Unrighteousness, "back him, you fool." The best efforts were made to screen him. People wrote him anonymous letters and warned him; but he would cheat, and they were obliged to find him out. Since that day, when my lord's shame was made public, the gaming-table has lost all its splendour. Shabby Jews and blacklegs prowl about racecourses and tavern parlours, and now and then inveigle silly yokels with greasy packs of cards in railroad ears; but Play is a deposed goddess, her worshippers bankrupt, and her table in rags.

So is another famous British institution gone to decay—the Ring: the noble practice of British boxing, which in my youth was still almost flourishing.

The prince, in his early days, was a great patron of this national sport, as his grand-uncle Culloden Cumberland had been before him; but, being present at a fight at Brighton, where one of the combatants was killed, the prince pensioned the boxer's widow, and declared he never would attend another battle. "But, nevertheless,"—I read in the noble language of Pierce Egan (whose smaller work on Pugilism I have the honour to possess),—"he thought it a manly and decided English feature, which ought not to be destroyed. His majesty had a drawing of the sporting characters in the Fives Court placed in his boudoir, to remind him of his former attachment and support of true courage; and when any fight of note occurred after he was king, accounts of it were read to him by his desire." That gives one a fine image of a king taking his recreation;—at ease in a royal dressing-gown;—too majestic to read himself, ordering the prime minister to read him accounts of battles: how Cribb punched Molyneux's eye, or Jack Randall thrashed the Game Chicken.

Where my prince did actually distinguish himself was in driving. He drove once in four hours and a half from Brighton to Carlton House—fifty-six miles. All the young men of that day were fond of that sport. But the fashion of rapid driving deserted England; and, I believe, trotted over to America. Where are the amusements of our youth? I hear of no gambling now but amongst obscure ruffians; of no boxing but amongst the lowest rabble. One solitary four-in-hand still drove round the parks in London last year; but that charioteer must soon disappear. He was very old; he was attired after the fashion of the year 1825. He must drive to the banks of Styx ere long,—where the ferry-boat waits to carry him over to the defunct revellers, who boxed and gambled and drank and drove with King George.

The bravery of the Brunswicks, that all the family must have it, that George possessed it, are points which all English writers have agreed to admit; and yet I cannot see how George IV should have been endowed with this quality. Swaddled in feather-beds all his life, lazy, obese, perpetually eating and drinking, his education was quite unlike that of his tough old progenitors. His grandsires had confronted hardship and war, and ridden up and fired their pistols undaunted into the face of death. His father had conquered luxury, and overcome indolence. Here was one who never resisted any temptation; never had a desire but he coddled and pampered it; if ever he had any nerve, frittered it away among cooks, and tailors, and barbers, and furniture-mongers, and opera dancers. What muscle would not grow flaccid in such a life—a life that was never strung up to any action—an endless Capua without any campaign—all fiddling, and flowers, and feasting, and flattery, and folly? When George III was pressed by the Catholic question and the India Bill, he said he would retire to Hanover rather than yield upon either point; and he would have done what he said. But, before yielding, he was determined to fight his ministers and Parliament; and he did, and he beat them. The time came when George IV was pressed too upon the Catholic claims: the cautious Peel had slipped over to that side; the grim old Wellington had joined it; and Peel tells us, in his Memoirs, what was the conduct of the king. He at first refused to submit; whereupon Peel and the duke offered their resignations, which their gracious master accepted. He did these two gentlemen the honour, Peel says, to kiss them both when they went away. (Fancy old Arthur's grim countenance and eagle beak as the monarch kisses it!) When they were gone he sent after them, surrendered, and wrote to them a letter begging them to remain in office, and allowing them to have their way. Then his Majesty had a meeting with Eldon, which is related at curious length in the latter's Memoirs. He told Eldon what was not true about his interview with the new Catholic converts; utterly misled the old ex-chancellor; cried, whimpered, fell on his neck, and kissed him too. We know old Eldon's own tears were pumped very freely. Did these two fountains gush together? I can't fancy a behaviour more unmanly, imbecile, pitiable. This a Defender of the Faith! This a chief in the crisis of a great nation! This an inheritor of the courage of the Georges! Many of my hearers no doubt have journeyed to the pretty old town of Brunswick, in company with that most worthy, prudent, and polite gentleman, the Earl of Malmesbury, and fetched away Princess Caroline for her longing husband, the Prince of Wales, Old Queen Charlotte would have had her eldest son marry a niece of her own, that famous Louisa of Strelitz, afterwards Queen of Prussia, and who shares with Marie Antoinette in the last age the sad pre-eminence of beauty and misfortune. But George III had a niece at Brunswick: she was a richer princess than her Serene Highness of Strelitz:—in fine, the Princess Caroline was selected to marry the heir to the English throne. We follow my Lord Malmesbury in quest of her; we are introduced to her illustrious father and royal mother; we witness the balls and fêtes of the old Court; we are presented to the princess herself, with her fair hair, her blue eyes, and her impertinent shoulders—a lively, bouncing, romping princess, who takes the advice of her courtly English mentor most generously and kindly. We can be present at her very toilette, if we like, regarding which, and for very good reasons, the British courtier implores her to be particular. What a strange Court! What a queer privacy of morals and manners do we look into! Shall we regard it as preachers and moralists, and cry, Woe, against the open vice and selfishness and corruption; or look at it as we do at the king in the pantomime, with his pantomime wife, and pantomime courtiers, whose big heads he knocks together, whom he pokes with his pantomime sceptre, whom he orders to prison under the guard of his pantomime beefeaters, as he sits down to dine on his pantomime pudding? It is grave, it is sad, it is theme most curious for moral and political speculation; it is monstrous, grotesque, laughable, with its prodigious littlenesses, etiquettes, ceremonials, sham moralities; it is as serious as a sermon, and as absurd and outrageous as Punch's puppet-show.

Malmesbury tells us of the private life of the duke, Princess Caroline's father, who was to die, like his warlike son, in arms against the French; presents us to his courtiers, his favourite; his duchess, George III's sister, a grim old princess, who took the British envoy aside, and told him wicked old stories of wicked old dead people and times; who came to England afterwards when her nephew was regent, and lived in a shabby furnished lodging, old, and dingy, and deserted, and grotesque, but somehow royal. And we go with him to the duke to demand the princess's hand in form, and we hear the Brunswick guns fire their adieux of salute, as H.R.H. the Princess of Wales departs in the frost and snow; and we visit the domains of the Prince Bishop of Osnaburg—the Duke of York of our early time; and we dodge about from the French revolutionists, whose ragged legions are pouring over Holland and Germany, and gaily trampling down the old world to the tune of Ça ira; and we take shipping at Slade, and we land at Greenwich, where the princess's ladies and the prince's ladies are in waiting to receive her royal highness.

What a history follows! Arrived in London, the bridegroom hastened eagerly to receive his bride. When she was first presented to him, Lord Malmesbury says she very properly attempted to kneel. He raised her gracefully enough, embraced her, and turning round to me, said,—

"Harris, I am not well; pray get me a glass of brandy."

I said, "Sir, had you not better have a glass of water?"

Upon which, much out of humour, he said, with an oath, "No; I will go to the queen."

What could be expected from a wedding which had such a beginning—from such a bridegroom and such a bride? I am not going to carry you through the scandal of that story, or follow the poor princess through all her vagaries; her balls and her dances, her travels to Jerusalem and Naples, her jigs, and her junketings, and her tears. As I read her trial in history, I vote she is not guilty. I don't say it is an impartial verdict; but as one reads her story the heart bleeds for the kindly, generous, outraged creature. If wrong there be, let it lie at his door who wickedly thrust her from it. Spite of her follies, the great, hearty people of England loved, and protected, and pitied her. "God bless you! we will bring your husband back to you," said a mechanic one day, as she told Lady Charlotte Bury with tears streaming down her cheeks. They could not bring that husband back; they could not cleanse that selfish heart. Was hers the only one he had wounded? Steeped in selfishness, impotent for faithful attachment and manly enduring love,— had it not survived remorse, was it not accustomed to desertion?

Malmesbury gives us the beginning of the marriage story;—how the prince reeled into chapel to be married; how he hiccupped out his vows of fidelity—you know how he kept them; how he pursued the woman whom he had married; to what a state he brought her; with what blows he struck her; with what malignity he pursued her; what his treatment of his daughter was; and what his own life. He the first gentleman of Europe! There is no stronger satire on the proud English society of that day, than that they admired George.

No, thank God, we can tell of better gentlemen; and whilst our eyes turn away, shocked, from this monstrous image of pride, vanity, weakness, they may see in that England over which the last George pretended to reign, some who merit indeed the title of gentlemen, some who make our hearts beat when we hear their names, and whose memory we fondly salute when that of yonder imperial manikin is tumbled into oblivion. I will take men of my own profession of letters. I will take Walter Scott, who loved the king, and who was his sword and buckler, and championed him like that brave Highlander in his own story, who fights round his craven chief. What a good gentleman! What a friendly soul, what a generous hand, what an amiable life was that of the noble Sir Walter! I will take another man of letters, whose life I admire even more,—an English worthy, doing his duty for fifty noble years of labour, day by day storing up learning, day by day working for scant wages, most charitable out of his small means, bravely faithful to the calling which he had chosen, refusing to turn from his path for popular praise or princes' favour;—I mean Robert Southey. We have left his old political landmarks miles and miles behind; we protest against his dogmatism; nay, we begin to forget it and his politics: but I hope his life will not be forgotten, for it is sublime in its simplicity, its energy, its honour, its affection. In the combat between Time and Thalaba, I suspect the former destroyer has conquered. Kehama's curse frightens very few readers now; but Southey's private letters are worth piles of epics, and are sure to last among us, as long as kind hearts like to sympathize with goodness and purity, and love and upright life. "If your feelings are like mine," he writes to his wife, "I will not go to Lisbon without you, or I will stay at home, and not part from you. For though not unhappy when away, still without you I am not happy. For your sake, as well as my own and little Edith's, I will not consent to any separation; the growth of a year's love between her and me, if it please God she should live, is a thing too delightful in itself, and too valuable in its consequences, to be given up for any light inconvenience on your part or mine.... On these things we will talk at leisure; only, dear, dear Edith, we must not part!"

This was a poor literary gentleman. The First Gentleman in Europe had a wife and daughter too. Did he love them so? Was he faithful to them? Did he sacrifice ease for them, or show them the sacred examples of religion and honour? Heaven gave the Great English Prodigal no such good fortune. Peel proposed to make a baronet of Southey; and to this advancement the king agreed. The poet nobly rejected the offered promotion.

"I have," he wrote, "a pension of 200 l. a year, conferred upon me by the good offices of my old friend C. Wynn, and I have the laureateship. The salary of the latter was immediately appropriated, as far as it went, to a life insurance for 3,000 l., which, with an earlier insurance, is the sole provision I have made for my family. All beyond must be derived from my own industry. Writing for a livelihood, a livelihood is all that I have gained; for, having also something better in view, and never, therefore, having courted popularity, nor written for the mere sake of gain, it has not been possible for me to lay by anything. Last year, for the first time in my life, I was provided with a year's expenditure beforehand. This exposition may show how unbecoming and unwise it would be to accept the rank which, so greatly to my honour, you have solicited for me."

How noble his poverty is, compared to the wealth of his master! His acceptance even of a pension was made the object of his opponents' satire: but think of the merit and modesty of this state pensioner; and that other enormous drawer of public money, who receives 100,000 l. a year, and comes to Parliament with a request for 650,000 l. more!

Another true knight of those days was Cuthbert Collingwood; and I think, since Heaven made gentlemen, there is no record of a better one than that. Of brighter deeds, I grant you, we may read performed by others; but where of a nobler, kinder, more beautiful life of duty, of a gentler, truer heart? Beyond dazzle of success and blaze of genius, I fancy shining a hundred and a hundred times higher, the sublime purity of Collingwood's gentle glory. His heroism stirs British hearts when we recall it. His love, and goodness, and piety make one thrill with happy emotion. As one reads of him and his great comrade going into the victory with which their names are immortally connected, how the old English word comes up, and that old English feeling of what I should like to call Christian honour! What gentlemen they were, what great hearts they had! "We can, my dear Coll," writes Nelson to him, "have no little jealousies; we have only one great object in view,—that of meeting the enemy, and getting a glorious peace for our country." At Trafalgar, when the Royal Sovereign was pressing alone into the midst of the combined fleets, Lord Nelson said to Captain Blackwood: "See how that noble fellow Collingwood takes his ship into action! How I envy him!" The very same throb and impulse of heroic generosity was beating in Collingwood's honest bosom. As he led into the fight, he said: "What would Nelson give to be here!"

After the action of the 1st of June, he writes:—"We cruised for a few days, like disappointed people looking for what they could not find, until the morning of little Sarah's birthday, between eight and nine o'clock, when the French fleet, of twenty-five sail of the line, was discovered to windward. We chased them, and they bore down within about five miles of us. The night was spent in watching and preparation for the succeeding day; and many a blessing did I send forth to my Sarah, lest I should never bless her more. At dawn, we made our approach on the enemy, then drew up, dressed our ranks, and it was about eight when the admiral made the signal for each ship to engage her opponent, and bring her to close action; and then down we went under a crowd of sail, and in a manner that would have animated the coldest heart, and struck terror into the most intrepid enemy. The ship we were to engage was two ahead of the French admiral, so we had to go through his fire and that of two ships next to him, and received all their broadsides two or three times, before we fired a gun. It was then near ten o'clock. I observed to the admiral, that about that time our wives were going to church, but that I thought the peal we should ring about the Frenchman's ears would outdo their parish bells."

There are no words to tell what the heart feels in reading the simple phrases of such a hero. Here is victory and courage, but love sublimer and superior. Here is a Christian soldier spending the night before battle in watching and preparing for the succeeding day, thinking of his dearest home, and sending many blessings forth to his Sarah, "lest he should never bless her more." Who would not say Amen to his supplication? It was a benediction to his country—the prayer of that intrepid loving heart.

We have spoken of a good soldier and good men of letters as specimens of English gentlemen of the age just past: may we not also—many of my elder hearers, I am sure, have read, and fondly remember his delightful story—speak of a good divine, and mention Reginald Heber as one of the best of English gentlemen? The charming poet, the happy possessor of all sorts of gifts and accomplishments, birth, wit, fame, high character, competence—he was the beloved parish priest in his own home of Hoderel, "counselling his people in their troubles, advising them in their difficulties, comforting them in distress, kneeling often at their sick-beds at the hazard of his own life; exhorting, encouraging where there was need; where there was strife the peacemaker; where there was want the free giver."

When the Indian bishopric was offered to him he refused at first; but after communing with himself (and committing his case to the quarter whither such pious men are wont to carry their doubts), he withdrew his refusal, and prepared himself for his mission and to leave his beloved parish. "Little children, love one another, and forgive one another," were the last sacred words he said to his weeping people. He parted with them, knowing, perhaps, he should see them no more. Like those other good men of whom we have just spoken, love and duty were his life's aim. Happy he, happy they who were so gloriously faithful to both! He writes to his wife those charming lines on his journey:—

If thou, my love, wert by my side, my babies at my knee,
How gladly would our pinnace glide o'er Gunga's mimic sea!

I miss thee at the dawning grey, when, on our deck reclined,
In careless ease my limbs I lay and woo the cooler wind.

I miss thee when by Gunga's stream my twilight steps I guide;
But most beneath the lamp's pale beam I miss thee by my side.

I spread my books, my pencil try, the lingering noon to cheer;
But miss thy kind approving eye, thy meek attentive ear.

But when of morn and eve the star beholds me on my knee,
I feel, though thou art distant far, thy prayers ascend for me.

Then on! then on! where duty leads my course be onward still,—
O'er broad Hindostan's sultry meads, o'er bleak Almorah's hill.

That course nor Delhi's kingly gates, nor wild Malwah detain,
For sweet the bliss us both awaits by yonder western main.

Thy towers, Bombay, gleam bright, they say, across the dark blue sea:
But ne'er were hearts so blithe and gay as there shall meet in thee!

Is it not Collingwood and Sarah, and Southey and Edith? His affection is part of his life. What were life without it? Without love, I can fancy no gentleman.

How touching is a remark Heber makes in his Travels through India, that on inquiring of the natives at a town, which of the governors of India stood highest in the opinion of the people, he found that, though Lord Wellesley and Warren Hastings were honoured as the two greatest men who had ever ruled this part of the world, the people spoke with chief affection of Judge Cleaveland, who had died, aged twenty-nine, in 1784. The people have built a monument over him, and still hold a religious feast in his memory. So does his own country still tend with a heart's regard the memory of the gentle Heber.

And Cleaveland died in 1784, and is still loved by the heathen, is he? Why, that year 1784 was remarkable in the life of our friend the First Gentleman of Europe. Do you not know that he was twenty-one in that year, and opened Carlton House with a grand ball to the nobility and gentry, and doubtless wore that lovely pink coat which we have described. I was eager to read about the ball, and looked to the old magazines for information. The entertainment took place on the 10th February. In the European Magazine of March, 1784, I came straightway upon it:—

"The alterations at Carlton House being finished, we lay before our readers a description of the state apartments as they appeared on the 10th instant, when H.R.H. gave a grand ball to the principal nobility and gentry.... The entrance to the state room fills the mind with an inexpressible idea of greatness and splendour.

"The state chair is of a gold frame, covered with crimson damask; on each corner of the feet is a lion's head, expressive of fortitude and strength; the feet of the chair have serpents twining round them, to denote wisdom. Facing the throne, appears the helmet of Minerva; and over the windows, glory is represented by St. George with a superb gloria.

"But the saloon may be styled the chef-d'œuvre, and in every ornament discovers great invention. It is hung with a figured lemon satin. The window-curtains, sofas, and chairs are of the same colour. The ceiling is ornamented with emblematical paintings, representing the Graces and Muses, together with Jupiter, Mercury, Apollo, and Paris. Two ormolu chandeliers are placed here. It is impossible by expression to do justice to the extraordinary workmanship, as well as design, of the ornaments. They each consist of a palm, branching out in five directions for the reception of lights. A beautiful figure of a rural nymph is represented entwining the stems of the tree with wreaths of flowers. In the centre of the room is a rich chandelier. To see this apartment dans son plus beau jour, it should be viewed in the glass over the chimney-piece. The range of apartments from the saloon to the ballroom, when the doors are open, formed one of the grandest spectacles that ever was beheld."

In the Gentleman's Magazine, for the very same month and year—March, 1784—is an account of another festival, in which another great gentleman of English extraction is represented as taking a principal share:—

"According to order, H.E. the Commander-in-Chief was admitted to a public audience of Congress; and, being seated, the president, after a pause, informed him that the United States assembled were ready to receive his communications. Whereupon he arose, and spoke as follows:—

"'Mr. President,—The great events on which my resignation depended having at length taken place, I present myself before Congress to surrender into their hands the trust committed to me, and to claim the indulgence of retiring from the service of my country.

"'Happy in the confirmation of our independence and sovereignty, I resign the appointment I accepted with diffidence; which, however, was superseded by a confidence in the rectitude of our cause, the support of the supreme power of the nation, and the patronage of Heaven. I close this last act of my official life, by commending the interests of our dearest country to the protection of Almighty God, and those who have the superintendence of them to His holy keeping. Having finished the work assigned me, I retire from the great theatre of action; and, bidding an affectionate farewell to this august body, under whose orders I have so long acted, I here offer my commission and take my leave of the employments of my public life.' To which the President replied:—

"'Sir, having defended the standard of liberty in the New World, having taught a lesson useful to those who inflict and those who feel oppression, you retire with the blessings of your fellow citizens; though the glory of your virtues will not terminate with your military command, but will descend to remotest ages.'"

Which was the most splendid spectacle ever witnessed:—the opening feast of Prince George in London, or the resignation of Washington? Which is the noble character for after-ages to admire;—yon fribble dancing in lace and spangles, or yonder hero who sheathes his sword after a life of spotless honour, a purity unreproached, a courage indomitable, and a consummate victory? Which of these is the true gentleman? What is it to be a gentleman? Is it to have lofty aims, to lead a pure life, to keep your honour virgin; to have the esteem of your fellow citizens, and the love of your fireside; to bear good fortune meekly; to suffer evil with constancy; and through evil or good to maintain truth always? Show me the happy man whose life exhibits these qualities, and him we will salute as gentleman, whatever his rank may be; show me the prince who possesses them, and he may be sure of our love and loyalty. The heart of Britain still beats kindly for George III,—not because he was wise and just, but because he was pure in life, honest in intent, and because according to his lights he worshipped Heaven. I think we acknowledge in the inheritrix of his sceptre, a wiser rule, and a life as honourable and pure; and I am sure the future painter of our manners will pay a willing allegiance to that good life, and be loyal to the memory of that unsullied virtue.

William Makepeace Thackeray – A Short Biography

William Makepeace Thackeray, was born on July 18th, 1811 in Calcutta, then British India, where his father, Richmond Thackeray was the secretary to the Board of Revenue in the British East India Company. His mother, Anne Becher also worked for the British East India Company.

His father died in 1815, and his mother sent Thackeray to England the following year while she remained in India and would, sometime later, marry her childhood sweetheart. En-route to England the ship stopped for provisions on St. Helena. The Imprisoned Napoleon was pointed out to him by a servant with the words that he "eats three sheep every day, and all the little children he can lay hands on!"

Finally, back in England the young Thackeray was sent to school, initially in Southampton and Chiswick, before being moved to Charterhouse School. Charterhouse and Thackeray did not take to each other but the time became a valuable source for his later work "Slaughterhouse". Despite his less than respectful recalling of his time with them Charterhouse placed a monument in the chapel after his death.

In his final year at Charterhouse a troubling illness delayed his departure to attend Cambridge University. Over the course of his life Thackeray would suffer from ill health, much of it brought about for his fondness for "gluttling and gorging". Excess was something he could enjoy and for a man who stood some 6' 3" it would appear to the eye that, initially at least, his large frame could absorb much of that excess.

However, Thackeray's lazy attitude to completely mastering anything he set his mind too, especially where ambition for academia was involved, meant he departed Cambridge little more than a year after joining. He had however published two short works in University periodicals. As an author, he would have quite some impact on English literature in the years to come, so it seems difficult to reconcile that he felt no urgency to pursue writing at that time.

He now spent some time travelling across Europe stopping at both Paris, to study art, and to winter in Weimar. Back in London a final attempt was made on a professional career. This time studying law at Middle Temple. It lasted no more than a few months.

Now, having reached 21, he received his father's inheritance. It was a very substantial estate of 17,000 pounds, an enormous sum of money at the time. However, although Thackeray had youth he lacked a little in energy and certainly much financial experience. He funded not one but two newspapers, and neither was to prove successful. Gambling seemed enjoyable and certainly he had money to lose, which he did on a regular basis. Further investments in two soon-to-fail Indian banks quickly ensured little of his good fortune remained.

He now had to consider taking up yet another profession. Thackeray turned to art hoping that his studies in Paris would prove of benefit. Unfortunately, they did not. His ambivalent attitude continued until on August 20th, 1836 he married the 20-year-old, Isabella Gethin Shawe. It seemed to prove a turning point in many ways.

The marriage would produce three daughters; Anne Isabella in 1837, Jane, in 1838, who tragically died in infancy and Harriet Marian in 1840.

Now, as a husband and father, Thackeray seemed at last to understand his responsibilities to nurture and provide.

His early efforts at "writing for his life" were to establish his career as a foremost author. His main employment was with Fraser's Magazine, a sharp-witted and sharp-tongued conservative publication for which he produced art criticism, short fictional sketches, and who would also serialise two of his novels. He also found time, between 1837 and 1840 to review books for The Times and to make regular contributions to The Morning Chronicle and The Foreign Quarterly Review.

In his earliest works, which he wrote under various pseudonyms including; Charles James Yellowplush, Michael Angelo Titmarsh and George Savage Fitz-Boodle, he tended towards savagery in his attacks on high society, military prowess, the institution of marriage and hypocrisy.

Between May 1839 and February 1840 Fraser's published Catherine. Originally intended as a satire of the Newgate school of crime fiction, it ended up being more of a picaresque tale. Thackeray also began work on what would eventually become A Shabby Genteel Story.

However, Thackeray, having successfully found a career that he cared about and had the talent for, found that his personal life was about to descend into chaos. After the birth of her third child in 1840, Isabella, sank into depression. At first Thackeray, didn't think too much of it. He needed to work to earn an income to support his family and finding that Isabella was distracting both herself and him he realised he could get no work done at home and so spent more and more time away until finally, in September 1840, it dawned upon him how serious his wife's condition had become. Struck by guilt, he set out with his wife to Ireland. During the boat crossing she threw herself into the sea, but was thankfully pulled from the waters. Her mother who had little understanding of her daughter's illness was of little help and perhaps a hinderance. After four-weeks they returned to England. From November 1840 to February 1842 Isabella was in and out of professional care, as her condition waxed and waned.

Isabella eventually deteriorated into a permanent state of detachment. Thackeray desperately sought cures for her, but nothing worked, and she ended up in two different asylums in or near Paris until 1845, after which Thackeray took her back to England, where he installed her with a Mrs Bakewell at Camberwell. Despite her condition Isabella would outlive her husband by 3 decades.

After his wife's illness Thackeray became a de facto widower, never able to establish another permanent relationship.

In 1843, through his connection to the illustrator John Leech, whom he had met at Charterhouse, he began writing for the newly created magazine Punch, in which he published The Snob Papers, later collected as The Book of Snobs. Thackeray was a regular contributor to Punch until 1854.

Thackeray had earlier received some success with two travel books, The Paris Sketch Book and The Irish Sketch Book, the latter marked by hostility to Irish Catholics. The book appealed to British prejudices, and on that basis Thackeray now became Punch's Irish expert, often under the pseudonym Hibernis Hibernior. It was Thackeray's writings that were the basis for Punch's notoriously harsh, hostile and condescending depictions of the Irish during the devastating Irish Famine (1845–51).

As well as his regular columns and contributions Thackeray worked on his novels. In The Luck of Barry Lyndon, which was serialised in Fraser's in 1844, he explored the situation of an outsider trying to achieve status in high society, a theme he developed more successfully a few years later with Vanity Fair.

Thackeray achieved more recognition with his Snob Papers (serialised 1846/7, and published as a book in 1848), but the work that really established his fame was the novel Vanity Fair, which first appeared in serialised instalments beginning in January 1847.

Published as a book the novel had a slow start but eventually sales rose to 7,000 copies a month. Just as importantly, it was the book that everybody was talking about. Thackeray finally had a name that gained notice and was reviewed in journals such as the famed, and much sought after, Edinburgh Review.

The accolades and success also gave him a respite from writing everything in a manner that would help ensure income rather than literary respect. Even before Vanity Fair completed its serial run Thackeray had become a celebrity, sought after by the very lords and ladies whom he satirised. with the character of Becky Sharp, the artist's daughter who rises high by manipulating all around her.

Pendennis followed in 1849-50, but it was interrupted halfway through writing for 3 months by a severe illness. Some accounts say it was cholera. Pendennis is a semi-autobiographical bildungsroman that draws on, among other things, Thackeray's disappointments in college, his ambivalent relationship with his mother, and his insider's knowledge of the London publishing world.

This novel ran at the same time as Charles Dicken's David Copperfield, and their dual appearance brought about the first of many comparisons with Dickens. Thackeray, for his part, felt that he and Dickens were battling for supremacy, though he would never equal Dickens's popularity, except with the critics.

Interestingly the two were involved in a spat which became known as the "Garrick Club affair". Thackeray and Dickens had skirmished over the "Dignity of Literature" and had other slight disagreements but this literary quarrel caused a rift in their friendship that lasted almost until the end of Thackeray's life. The relationship was healed only in Thackeray's last months, through a surprise meeting and handshake on the steps of a London club. Thackeray had taken offense at some personal remarks in a column by Edmund Yates and demanded an apology, eventually taking the affair to the Garrick Club committee. Already upset with Thackeray for an indiscreet remark about his affair with Ellen Ternan, Dickens championed Yates, helping him to write letters both to Thackeray and, in his defense, to the club's committee. Despite the intervention of Dickens, Yates eventually lost the vote of the Club's members, but the quarrel was laid out for the public in journal articles and pamphlets. "What pains me most," Thackeray said at the time, "is that Dickens should have been his adviser, and next that I should have had to lay a heavy hand on a young man who, I take it, has been cruelly punished by the issue of the affair, and I believe is hardly aware of the nature of his own offence, and doesn't even now understand that a gentleman should resent the monstrous insult which he volunteered".

Aside from these quarrelsome, distracting literary disagreements and Isabella's on-going illness life was good for Thackeray. He was to remain as he put it "at the top of the tree," for the rest of his life. The works for which he is so well remembered; Vanity Fair and Barry Lyndon had established that but he continued to write and produce novels, stories, sketches and works profusely.

To remain at such a high level in both quality and quantity is somewhat surprising given the continuation and escalation of various illnesses which continued to haunt him.

With Isabella still unwell Thackeray did seek out other women, in particular Mrs Jane Brookfield. Despite his hopes, it always felt that he was pursuing her as she battled the problems of her own marriage and turned to Thackeray for comfort and support. A source for these relationships often came on the lecture tours of Great Britain and the United States which he now entertained. These tours gave the public a chance to see and hear their hero's and provided another valuable source of income for those invited to tour. Whilst in in New York he met the Baxter family. Sally, the eldest daughter, enchanted the novelist—as a number of vibrant, intelligent, beautiful young women had done before her—and she became the model for Ethel Newcome. He visited her on his second tour of the States when she was married to a South Carolina gentleman. His choosing of married women in the shape of both Jane and Sally was ill-advised and both relationships led nowhere but did take quite some time to disassemble and for reason to set in.

In 1852, The History of Henry Esmond was published as a 3-volume novel without first being serialised and in a special type meant to imitate the appearance of an eighteenth-century book. This was the most carefully planned of Thackeray's novels. The book was celebrated for its brilliance, and Thackeray recognized it as "the very best I can do". At the time, it caused a sensation thanks to its controversial ending, wherein the hero marries a woman who early in the novel seemed more like a "mother" to him.

The eighteenth-century held a great attraction for Thackeray and he had previously set both Barry Lyndon and Catherine there as well as the sequel to Esmond, The Virginians, which takes place in North America and includes George Washington as a character.

Thackeray had twice visited the United States on lecture tours during this period as well as given lectures in London on the English humorists of the eighteenth century, and on the first four Hanoverian monarchs. The latter were published in a book as The Four Georges.

Interestingly Thackeray also decided that Politics was something he could more than dabble in. In Oxford he stood as an independent for Parliament. He was narrowly beaten by Cardwell, a politician who was substituted for the man Thackeray thought he was going to run against, although Thackeray's advocacy of entertainment on the Sabbath would have done little to help his campaign. Even so the margin of his defeat was only 1,070 votes, to Thackeray's 1,005.

In 1860 Thackeray became editor of the newly established Cornhill Magazine, a role he never felt truly comfortable in, preferring to contribute as a columnist on the Roundabout Papers. However, the financial compensation was by all accounts quite extraordinary. The Cornhill began its history with a record circulation and a number of distinguished contributors swayed onboard by Thackeray's reputation. It was in the Cornhill that he serialised his last complete novel, The Adventures of Philip in 1861-62. (After his death, the incomplete Denis Duval would also appear there in 1864).

After two years as editor he stepped down, primarily to concentrate on writing novels again. A piece he wrote for the Cornhill at this time "Thorns in the Cushion," one of The Roundabout Papers, fondly assembles the pains he felt in rejecting manuscripts on the one hand and receiving criticism of the magazine on the other. It seemed a good time to move on.

Thackeray's health had worsened during the 1850s and he was plagued by a recurring stricture of the urethra that laid him up for days at a time. He also felt that he had lost much of his creative impetus. He worsened matters by excessively eating and drinking, and avoiding exercise, though he enjoyed horseback-riding. He has been described as "the greatest literary glutton who ever lived". Indeed, his main activity apart from writing was eating and drinking and many of his stories include elaborate scenes and themes on his fondness for them.

On December 23rd, 1863, William Makepeace Thackeray, after returning from dining out and before dressing for bed, suffered a massive stroke. He was found dead on his bed the following morning. He was only fifty-two.

His death was entirely unexpected, and shocked family, friends and indeed the entire Nation.

It is said that at his funeral service thousands of mourners turned out to witness his passing. He was buried on December 29th at Kensal Green Cemetery, London.

William Makepeace Thackeray – A Concise Bibliography

The Yellowplush Papers (1837)
Catherine (1839–40)

A Shabby Genteel Story (1840)
Second Funeral of Napoleon (1841)
The Irish Sketchbook (1843)
The Luck of Barry Lyndon (1844)
Notes of a Journey from Cornhill to Grand Cairo (1846)
Mrs. Perkins's Ball (1846), under the name M. A. Titmarsh
Stray Papers: Being Stories, Reviews, Verses, and Sketches (1821-1847)
The Book of Snobs (1848)
Vanity Fair (1848)
Pendennis (1848–1850)
Rebecca and Rowena (1850)
The Paris Sketchbook (1840)
Men's Wives (1852)
The History of Henry Esmond (1852)
The English Humorists of the Eighteenth Century (1853)
The Newcomes (1855)
The Rose and the Ring (1855)
The Virginians (1857–1859)
Lovel the Widower (1860)
Four Georges (1860-1861)
The Adventures of Philip (1862)
Roundabout Papers (1863)
Denis Duval (1864)
The English Humorists of the eighteenth century: A Series of Six Lectures (1867)
Ballads (1869)
Burlesques (1869)
The Orphan of Pimlico (1876)

Thackeray wrote a numerous number of articles for magazines and the like as well as contributing many picture sketches to articles and his own books. Many were then collected and published together. We have listed his major works only for this bibliography.

www.ingramcontent.com/pod-product-compliance
Lightning Source LLC
Chambersburg PA
CBHW061455170626
46811CB00004B/1526